MURDER IN EUREKA SPRINGS
Three Novellas

MURDER AT DAIRY HOLLOW

MURDER AT THE
CRESCENT HOTEL

MURDER AT THE OZARK UFO
CONFERENCE

MARIELLEN GRIFFITH

Cahaba Press
Eureka Springs, Arkansas

Cahaba Press
483 County Road 231
Eureka Springs, AR 72631
USA
www.cahabapress.com

MURDER IN EUREKA SPRINGS:
Three Novellas

MURDER AT DAIRY HOLLOW

MURDER AT THE CRESCENT HOTEL

MURDER AT THE OZARK UFO CONFERENCE

ISBN-13: 978-1532824975

ISBN-10: 1532824971

Contents

MURDER AT DAIRY HOLLOW

Dedication

This book is dedicated to my fellow readers and writers who listen and make comments about my writings at the by-monthly Readers and Writers' Guild. I also dedicate this book to Don, my husband, who encourages me to write and publish.

Prologue

The setting for the story is Dairy Hollow House, once a country inn and restaurant in the Ozark Mountain community of Eureka Springs, Arkansas. Eureka Springs is one of two county seats for Carroll County. Because the city has steep, winding streets filled with Victorian-style cottages and manors, the entire city has been placed on the National Register of Historic Places. Dairy Hollow House was the first historical property to be reused for tourism purposes in 1980, opening as an inn and restaurant.

In 1998, the owners of Dairy Hollow House began the process of dissolving the inn, to create a non-profit organization called the Writers Colony at Dairy Hollow. The Colony is a residency program for writers, artists, composers, architect and chefs. The colony is open year-round. Meetings and weekend programs are offered through the year.

This book is the result of my experiences several years ago in the spring when I attended a week long Writers' Workshop at Dairy Hollow. The theme was: *How to Write a Murder Mystery*. Little did I know when I registered for the workshop that I would actually experience a murder mystery.

Chapter One

On an early spring morning in April, Janice Henry, a sixty-year-old woman, walked out of her house in Eureka Springs to go to her car. She was wearing her usual work outfit of blue jeans and a cotton shirt. She wore a scarf on her head, covering her hair, which was tied into a bun in the back. As she left her house, she became aware of the rising sun over East Mountain. The weather report for the day promised to be a high of seventy degrees. She looked forward to a beautiful and colorful spring day. She unlocked her car and drove to the Writers' Colony at Dairy Hollow, a ten minute drive from her home by way of Spring Street. She was happy to have a job since her husband had an accident and was confined to a wheelchair. Previous to working at the Writers' Colony, she had worked as a cook for Myrtie Mae's and Rowdy Beaver restaurants.

She parked her car in the Writers' Colony parking lot. As

she stepped out of her car she noticed that the Blue Bells and White Coral Bells were blooming. She sniffed the air and smiled. "It's going to be a beautiful day."

After work she planned to work in her own garden. She liked to grow herbs to add to the savory dishes that she would prepare for the meals at Dairy Hollow. She walked up the steps to the porch and opened the front door of the Dairy Hollow house with her key. She turned on the light on the right side of the door and hung her coat on an old wooden hall tree. As she was walking through the living and dining rooms, she thought about making a coffee cake and scrambling eggs for the attendees at the workshop today. As she stepped into the kitchen, she turned on the light and walked around the kitchen counter to turn on the coffee maker. There in the middle of the kitchen, next to the stove, was the body of a man lying in a pool of blood.

She began screaming and rushed out of the kitchen.

"What shall I do?" she said aloud. Her hands were shaking; she felt anxious and short of breath.

Then she reached for her cell phone and called 911. "Help, there's a dead body lying on the floor in a pool of blood at the Writers' Colony at Dairy Hollow! Please hurry!"

She paused, took a deep breath and then called the Executive Director, Joanna Reeves. "A man is lying in a pool of blood on the kitchen floor. I called 911 immediately. Please come!"

Janice sat in a chair and tried to get her breath under control. She thought she might faint.

The Sheriff and a Deputy arrived twenty minutes later with the Coroner following in his van. The Sheriff was wearing a police uniform and a badge. He was fifty-five years old, having worked as a policeman for the past thirty years. He had lived in Fayetteville until 2005 when he came to Eureka Springs to become the Sheriff. This was the first murder since he arrived, and he was not a happy man. The Deputy was thirty years old, having lived in Carroll County for most of his life. He received his police training in Fayetteville.

They found the body of a man lying on his back in a pool of blood.

"What happened here?" said the Sheriff to Janice.

"I don't know," said Janice, her voice quivering. "I am the cook. I ah . . . walked into the kitchen and saw the body on the floor. I screamed—I was so frightened. I didn't know what to do. I ran out of the kitchen and called 911 and . . ."

Just then Joanna walked into the kitchen interrupting Janice's comments.

"What's going on? Who was killed?" She bent over the body and gasped, "It's Sam Peters, the Writer-in-Residence here at the Writers' Colony. Oh my, how did this happen?" She leaned on the kitchen counter to brace herself.

"We don't know." said the Sheriff. "All we can tell is that he was stabbed. Joanna, let's sit at the table in the dining room and discuss what happened" He turned to the Deputy, "Go into the kitchen and look for clues and the murder weapon."

Following the Sherriff's comment, the Coroner said, "According to the rigor, the man has been dead for at least seven hours. Is it okay with you if we move the body?

"Yes, go ahead," said the Sheriff.

The Coroner and his crew removed the body and placed it in the Coroner's panel truck. Then they got into the truck and drove away.

After sitting down in a chair at the wooden dining table, the Sheriff said, "I have some questions to ask you."

"Go right ahead, Sheriff. I hope I can be helpful," said Joanna.

"First of all, tell me who is Sam Peters?" asked the Sheriff.

Joanna replied, "Sam is a writer from the suburbs of Chicago. He applied to us to become a Writer-In-Residence for this year, beginning in April. Also, we needed an instructor to co-teach a workshop for us. With Sam's background as a novelist and instructor, we asked him to teach the class, *How to Write a Murder Mystery*."

"Is there anything else that you can tell me?" asked the Sheriff. "Do you know anyone who would want to murder him?"

"No," responded Joanna. "Sam was well liked by all. He had excellent references."

"What was your relationship to him?" asked the Sheriff.

"Since I am the Executive Director of the Writers' Colony, I work with the Board Members to screen the applications from writers who are applying for a Writer-In-Residence position. We selected Sam Peters because of his extensive background in writing and teaching. He was highly regarded as a writer. We felt fortunate to have him."

"Did you know him personally?" asked the Sheriff.

"He had been here two and a half weeks. Often we had lunch or dinner together. We had become colleagues and friends. I respected him and admired him for his work."

"Thank you, Joanna; I want to make a copy of Sam's application to the Writers' Colony. Will you give me the file? We can talk at a later time after I have had time to read it." Joanna pushed her chair back, and stood up to get the file.

Chapter Two

With great excitement and nervous tension, I arrived at the Writers' Colony at Dairy Hollow in Eureka Springs after driving for one and one-half hours from Springfield, Missouri. As I parked my car and walked up the hill to the house, I became aware of the delightful aroma that rose from the flowers blooming along the sidewalk.

Helen, the registrar at Dairy Hollow, met me at the door and said, "My name is Helen; I am the registrar for the Writers' Workshop. Come in and sign the registration sheet."

We shook hands, and I said, "My name is Sue Henry; I live in Springfield, Missouri. I am so excited to be here."

"Welcome to the Writers' Colony at Dairy Hollow. Here is a folder with some workshop materials and a schedule. After you sign in, I will show you to your room where you will live for the week while attending the Writers'

Workshop."

We walked up the stairs to room number 5. I opened the door and turned around and said, "Thank you, Helen, I will see you later."

The room was small, but it had a large window overlooking a ravine of pine and cedar trees. A few hardwood trees were scattered throughout the ravine. The dogwood and redbud trees were in full bloom. The sun was shining in the east as it emerged over the Arkansas mountains on Monday morning.

Helen said that the workshop would start at 10:00 a.m. with lunch at 12:00. If I would like to have a cup of coffee, the kitchen was open. I unpacked my clothes and hung them in the small closet. I placed my notebook and registration materials on the bed so I wouldn't forget to take them with me to the workshop.

At 9:30 a.m. I walked downstairs and made my way through the Victorian sitting room to the kitchen to get a cup of coffee. Other workshop writers had arrived, and they were sitting around the dining room table drinking coffee and introducing themselves. I poured a cup of coffee and joined them. Normally, I'm shy and introverted, but I forced myself to smile and say, "Good morning." In my thoughts I wondered what I would say to these people. Will I come across as dumb and stupid? Will they think I don't belong at this workshop?

A loud, outspoken, middle-aged man wearing a suit and tie dominated the conversation. "My name is Simpson, Sam Simpson. I work in a bank. I have come all the way from New Jersey. I have always wanted to be a murder mystery writer, so here I am. I have written a few stories, but I've never written a murder mystery."

"Here is your chance," said a thin man over six-feet tall, who was wearing a blue shirt over a white t-shirt and jeans. "I don't think your bank experiences will prepare you to be a murder mystery writer. I have a college degree in Forensics. I have visited morgues and have seen dead bodies. I have attended other writers' workshops. I know that I am prepared to write a murder mystery story."

A tall, dark haired woman walked into the room and asked everyone to take a seat in the living room. After everyone was seated, she said, "I am Joanna Reeves. I'm the Executive Director of the Writers' Colony. I wish to introduce the instructors of this workshop. Jane Foster Mason, who many of you know as J.F. Mason, is seated near the fireplace. She has been a professional murder mystery writer for the last twenty years. Presently she lives in California. The other instructor is Sam Peters, who is sitting to my left. Sam is a Writer-In-Residence at the Writers' Colony and comes from the Chicago area. He has published a murder mystery novel and some short stories. He also has experience teaching."

"Thank you," said Sam and Jane.

"We are pleased to be here." Jane said, "First of all, I would like everyone to introduce themselves and tell us why you are here. Let's start with the person to my right and go around the room." Seated next to her was a petite blond middle-aged woman.

"My name is Sally Sanders. I'm a housewife, living in Rogers, and have raised three children who are all in college. I have always preferred reading mystery books. I am here because I would like to learn how to write one."

"Thank you, Sally," said Jane, "You will have that opportunity."

Seated next to Sally was a middle-aged male with a receding hairline, wearing a Western shirt and cowboy boots. "My name is Gary Nelson. I'm from Little Rock. I have written some Western cowboy stories with the help of my wife who edits my writing; but now I am interested in writing a murder mystery. I hope to gain some ideas at this workshop."

An older woman in her seventies spoke next. "My name is Donna Rizman. I am a retired office manager. My husband and I live in a retirement village in Oklahoma. We have been married for fifty years. I've written short stories, but never a murder mystery. I hope to learn a lot."

Next to Donna, was a young man wearing worn blue jeans and a blue shirt over a white t-shirt. He was sitting with a straight back and began speaking in a superior voice. "I am Woody Wilson. I have attended the Iowa Writers' School and have published several short stories. Now, I would like to write a murder mystery book and have it published."

"Your voice sounds familiar," said Sam to Woody. "Have we met?"

"Yes, I attended one of your lectures at a writers' workshop," said Woody.

The next person to speak was a portly middle-aged man who wore a suit and tie. He spoke in a loud voice. "I'm Ted Simpson, a banker, and I've been married for twenty years. I'm from New Jersey. I prefer reading mystery stories and watching PBS television mystery shows. I'm excited about learning how to write a mystery novel."

I was the last person to speak. I was so nervous and anxious. I took a deep breath and said, "Sue Henry is my name. I completed a degree in Sociology ten years ago after my kids finished high school. I decided I would rather write mysteries than become a teacher or social worker. I have read many mystery novels, but I haven't begun to write. I am looking forward to this workshop."

Murder at Dairy Hollow

"Thank you all for coming," said Jane Foster. "I hope that your expectations will be met. I am glad that many of you have read many murder mysteries. Already you have gathered some ideas about how murders are solved. But first, let me introduce myself. I am assuming that you have read my bio in the publicity for this workshop. To add to that bio, I want all of you to know that I did not originally want to become a writer. In college, I studied psychology and wanted to become a psychologist. However, my parents were killed in an automobile accident when I was a senior. I took a semester off, and then came back to finish my senior year. Not having my parents to support me, I went home and took a job at a local newspaper.

After a few years, I was asked to write news articles for the paper. I found out that I was good at writing. I began writing features and really enjoyed that. On the side, I began writing short stories. I attended a writing class at the local community college, and I've also attended writers' workshops in California. In the meantime, I was married for a few years and then got divorced. I began submitting short stories to magazines, and they were published. Then I began writing murder mystery novels, which were published. I like writing novels that have a psychological twist to the story. In summary, we all have to start somewhere—write and then write some more; through experience you will soon become a published writer."

"Thank you, Jane, that's quite an act to follow," said Sam. "I'm from Illinois. I have a degree in writing from the University of Illinois. After college, I worked at a publishing company as an editor for ten years. I was able to write at home in the evenings and on weekends. After several years I finally had a short story that was published. I must have written at least ten short stories before one of them was published. I put several of the short stories together, making changes here and there, and they became a novel. To my surprise, the novel was published. Don't give up if you receive rejection slips. Learn from your mistakes."

Jane spoke, "Thanks Sam for sharing. Here's a schedule of topics that we will be presenting." She passed the schedule to the participants and began reading the topics.

"I call the first topic the 'Basics'. You will need to answer the following questions: First, who is the detective? Second, who was murdered? Third, why was the person murdered? Fourth, how was the person murdered? Fifth, who are the suspects? And Sixth, who was the murderer? After you have answered those questions, write out the details. Make character profiles to remind you of who's who. Write down some lines, some phrases and some possible endings you might use. Now, spend the rest of the morning to begin answering these questions. If you need help or have any questions, Sam and I will be available."

Sam said, "Remember, stay focused on what you are writing."

Everyone began writing, except me. I froze. I don't know what to write, I thought. Now, they really will know how stupid I am. I took several deep breaths and tried to relax. Suddenly a thought came into my mind. I will have a female detective in my story whose name would be Jamey Summerville. Her sidekick would be called Wally Jones. The murder victim would be a man who just walked out of a bar in Springfield. He was murdered with a knife. The suspects were people in the bar. The murderer was a debt collector associated with a Loan Shark. I began to write as fast as I could before time would be called. Ten minutes later, Jane called time.

"Time is up," announced Jane, "and lunch is ready. Put your writing materials and books away, and come back at 1:00."

Quickly, I ran up the stairs to my room to put away my notebook. I washed my hands in the bathroom down the hall and ran back downstairs. As I walked through the dining room, I noticed that a line had formed in the kitchen and people were helping themselves to a buffet. In the buffet were salad materials, such as lettuce, tomatoes, cabbage slaw, cottage cheese and onions. Cold ham and bread were set out on different plates. We had the choice of either making a salad with the ham, or making a ham sandwich. I chose to make a salad. At the dining room table I sat next to Sally. We discussed the ages of our children and where they were going to school. After we finished eating, we took our dishes to the kitchen counter. To Janice, the cook, I said, "Thanks for a good lunch. The ham was delicious."

At 1:00 Sam called us into the living room for the afternoon meeting. After we sat down, he said, "Now that you have answered the questions from the morning session, you are ready to start writing the story." He handed out a sheet with directions for writing a story.

"There are ten sections. First write the opener; Second, the murder; Third, discovery of the body; Fourth, bring the suspects in; Fifth, the plot; Sixth, list the suspects; Seventh, thicken the plot even more; Eighth, rule the suspects down; Ninth, add clues to the story; and Tenth, write the ending. What kind of ending will you have? Is it a cliffhanger? Is there a confession? Now that you have answered all those questions, you are beginning to develop a story. Are there any other questions?"

With his brow furrowed, Steve said, "Yes, I have a question. Can we do all of this writing in just a week?"

Jane said, "You are not the only person who has asked that question in other workshops, Steve. You may think that we are asking a lot from all of you, but remember we have a week to sketch out these questions and ideas. We will assist all of you to complete this exercise. Are there any other questions? Around 3:00 let's take a 15-minute coffee break, and meet back here at 3:15. Sam and I will be walking around to each one of you to see how you're doing. Now, begin writing."

Chapter Three

Two weeks before the workshop began, Sam Peters was excited that his application to be a Writer-In-Residence at the Writers' Colony was accepted, and that he was asked to co-teach a murder mystery writing class at the Writers' Colony. Sam was forty-five years old, a professional writer, living in a Chicago suburb. He had sold a murder mystery novel and several short stories. Recently, his wife divorced him after ten years of marriage. She had fallen in love with another man who was rich and living in Chicago.

Sam needed to put his divorce behind him, and start a new life. This residency may be just what he needs. His residency started the first of April. On April 1st, the morning of his flight to Arkansas, he put on his best jeans, a short sleeved shirt and a corduroy jacket. He wanted to make a positive first impression by wearing a jacket. He even trimmed his dark beard. He flew on United Air Lines from Chicago to XNA. He had packed his clothes in a carry-on bag and put his hand written-notebook and computer in his briefcase. To Sam's relief, the plane left Chicago only a few minutes late and arrived on time in Bentonville, Arkansas.

Joanna, the Executive Director of the Writers' Colony, met him inside the airport. She was wearing dark slacks and a periwinkle colored blouse, which matched her eyes, under a dark jacket.

He noticed that she was sitting at a small table by a food and coffee stand drinking a cup of coffee. As he descended the escalator, he said to himself, "What an attractive woman, I wonder if she's single?" When Joanna saw him, she stood up and walked to greet him. They had previously exchanged photos through e-mail and were able to identify each other immediately. When they met, they shook hands.

"So nice to meet you," said Joanna. She thought to herself, he is handsome, and looks younger than his photo. Out loud she said, "How was your trip?"

Sam replied, "I am happy to be here. The airplane had a few bumps, but otherwise it was a smooth trip."

"Do you need to pick up any luggage?" said Joanna.

"No, I'm carrying my bag," said Sam.

"Then let's go to the car. It's that white Honda SUV,"

said Joanna. "Have you had lunch?"

"Yes, I had a sandwich on the plane," said Sam.

"Since we're in no hurry to reach the Writers' Colony, I would like to show you Crystal Bridges, a new American art museum in Bentonville. While there we can have coffee and dessert," said Joanna.

"Sounds good to me," said Sam. "I didn't know that there was a new art museum in Arkansas. Arkansas is not known for its art."

"You'll be surprised," said Joanna.

Once inside the car, Joanna turned the ignition on and the classical music station began playing a symphony by Beethoven. Joanna turned down the volume and said, "Do you like classical music?"

"This may sound a little trite, but I like the three Bs, Bach, Beethoven, and Brahms," replied Sam.

"What about the fourth 'B', inquired Joanna?

"Do you mean Bartok or Samuel Barber? I like *Serenade for Strings* by Barber and *Concerto for Orchestra* by Bartok,'" said Sam.

"I am impressed," said Joanna. "Few people that I know appreciate Bartok or Barber."

"Living so close to Chicago, my former wife and I had tickets to the Chicago Symphony and Lyric Opera for ten years," said Sam. "I learned to appreciate many composers and their music not usually played."

"You are fortunate," replied Joanna, "However, we have a small summer opera season performed by students. If we wish to attend a symphony concert, we have to drive over an hour to Fayetteville, the home of the University of Arkansas."

Joanna turned off the interstate to take the road to Crystal Bridges. As she was driving through the park like setting, Sam said, "What a beautiful natural area. The museum seems to have been built in a native arboretum."

"Actually, the area is natural. It was owned by the Walton family, owners of Walmart. The daughter, Alice Walton, is the founder of this museum. The goal is to plant and grow all native Arkansas plants and trees." Arriving at the museum parking lot, Joanna said, "Now, that we have arrived at the museum, I will park in the underground parking lot so we can take the elevator to the museum entrance."

For the next two hours Joanna and Sam toured the art museum and ended their tour with coffee and dessert at the Museum café.

"I am so surprised," said Sam. "I had no idea that such a place existed! Now I have a greater appreciation of American art. Thanks for bringing me to this museum, and I was surprised to learn that both of us do not understand contemporary art."

"I am pleased," said Joanna. "It seems that we have similar tastes in art, as well as in music. On the way home to Eureka Springs, we will have to discuss our interests in the literary world. We may differ."

"I look forward to that discussion," said Sam.

They left the museum and Joanna drove to Eureka Springs via Pea Ridge to Highway 62. Joanna shared the history of the Pea Ridge Civil War battle when they drove by the entrance to the park. For the next forty minutes, they discussed their favorite writers and books without any pauses. They realized that they had many common interests.

When they arrived at the Writers' Colony, Joanna parked in the parking lot and opened the door to the house with a key on her key chain. She showed Sam around the first floor, and then took him to the room where he would be staying for the next six months. Joanna left Sam to unpack, and get settled into his room. Before leaving, she said to him, "I hope you like your room and the view of the woods. The trees are natural to the Ozarks."

As Sam looked around the room and through the open window, he said, "This room is perfect and the setting is beautiful. I hope that I will not be distracted by the beauty and still be able to write."

"It may be difficult," replied Joanna. "Around six o'clock I will meet you in the living room, and we can go out to dinner at Local Flavor, one of my favorite restaurants in Eureka Springs. No meals are served here until the workshop begins in two weeks. There is a refrigerator in the kitchen where you can keep food."

She left him and drove to her home on the west side of Eureka Springs.

Sam unpacked his clothes, and hung them in a small closet. He put his books and writing materials on a desk overlooking a ravine. He decided to stretch out on the bed for a quick nap. He removed his shoes and jacket. He hung his jacket in the closet and put his shoes under the bed. He pulled back the hand stitched red and white quilt and lay down. Soon he was fast asleep. Sam slept for one hour. He awoke and checked his watch. The time was 5:30. Joanna will arrive at 6:00. He decided to shower and change clothes.

Joanna arrived promptly at 6:00. Sam was standing in the living room, looking out of the window when Joanna arrived. As soon as she drove into the parking lot, Sam walked out of the house and turned around to lock the door. Joanna saw him walk out of the house and unlocked the door on the passenger's side. Sam stepped off the porch and walked to the car, opened the door, and got in.

"Looks like you are ready to go," said Joanna.

Sam replied, "I'm starving. Where did you say we're going?"

Joanna drove out of the driveway onto Spring Street. She answered his question. "I'm driving to one of my favorite places in Eureka Springs, Local Flavor."

"Sounds good to me," said Sam. "Do they have steak?"

"We'll find out," said Joanna. She parked the car across the street. They walked into the restaurant and asked to be seated outdoors on the balcony.

The temperature was in the 70s, warm enough to sit outdoors. They ordered wine and drank it while reading the menu. Joanna ordered the fish of the day, and Sam ordered a sirloin steak with a baked potato. For the next hour they ate, talked, and drank more wine.

Around 8:00 Joanna took Sam back to the Writers' Colony and left him at the front door.

"Do you want to come in and stay awhile? Sam asked.

"I would like to, but I have work at home that I must take care of."

Sam got out of the car and watched Joanna drive off. He unlocked the door and walked up the stairs to his room. The evening was still early; he wasn't sleepy and didn't want to go to bed. He took out his notebook and pen from his briefcase, sat on the bed, reached over to the lamp on a bedside table and turned it on. He opened his notebook to an empty page and began to write. First, he wrote the date and time of the day. Then he began to describe the day. He had developed a habit of writing every evening in his notebook. He wrote about the events of the day, and people he had met. These notes helped him write stories based on his experiences. As he was writing and remembering what all happened that day, he thought that Joanna was a fascinating individual. Maybe he would put her in one of his stories. A couple of hours later, he put his notebook away, turned off the light and fell asleep.

Chapter Four

"Welcome to the second day of our Murder Mystery Workshop," said Jane Foster. "I hope you all slept well."

There were murmurs of "Yes" and "No" by the participants in the workshop, between sips of coffee.

Sam began speaking, "By now you have already started answering the questions that we gave you yesterday. Remember, that you need a mix of a complicated story and an easy one. It is okay to read other people's ideas to get inspired, but do not copy them. Since many of you are using a computer, remember to save your work as soon as you finish one paragraph. Are there any questions?"

Several people started talking at once. Ted Simpson's voice was the loudest and over talked the other people. He said, "Jane, how do you get started with writing a murder mystery, where do you get your ideas?"

"That's a good question," said Jane. "I do a lot of reading of police reports, news items in the paper, television, and on my IPad. Also, I have researchers on my staff to provide me with background for my novels."

"Okay, but I don't know where to go with my story. I have murdered a man in my story, but I haven't figured out who did it or what motive the murderer had," said Ted.

Sam said, "Let's brainstorm about the many possible ways a person could be murdered." Sam walked over to a whiteboard and wrote 'Ways to Murder' at the top of the board. "Remember," he said, "brainstorming means that all suggestions are accepted; we do not evaluate them."

There were many suggestions. Sam wrote them on the whiteboard: 'gun, bow and arrow, bomb, bashing the head with a board, poison, rifle, drowning, strangling, a knife.'

Donna spoke, "I saw an episode of NCIS where the Medical Examiner used a letter opener to make a wound in an artery in the arm, and the blood slowly bled out and the bad guy died."

"That's hard to believe," said Woody with a pompous voice. "I would like to create the perfect crime, where the murderer is not caught."

"Yes, you could write that story," said Jane, "but it doesn't follow the outline that we gave you."

"Do I have to follow your outline?" said Woody.

"If you wish to have your work published," said Jane. "Editors and publishers of murder mysteries like to publish novels or short stories that follow that outline."

Sam spoke, "If you want to write the perfect murder mystery, you can always write an epilogue from the murderer's viewpoint, describing his or her motive and means. I have read some novels that ended the story in that manner."

"We are here to teach you the basics of writing a murder mystery," said Jane. "If you think you know the basics of writing, then go ahead and write what you wish."

"Now wait one moment," Ted said angrily. "How can Woody get preferential treatment? Why can't he follow the directions like the rest of us? Who does he think he is?"

Woody jumped up and shook his fist at Ted and angrily responded, "I want you to know that I have attended other writers' workshops, and I know what I am doing!"

"Calm down, Woody, and please sit down. We can see that you're angered by Ted's comments. However, this is not the place or time to express your anger," said Sam. "Would you like to step outside for a while to cool down?"

Woody quickly left the room and walked outdoors. There was a long silence. Then Woody walked back into the room, sat down, and looked at Sam and Jane,

"I'm sorry that I lost my temper. I am here to learn. I

signed up for this workshop because there were going to be two professional writers teaching the workshop."

"Thank you, Woody. It takes courage to say what you did," said Sam. "Welcome back." To the group, Sam said, "It's normal for any of us to get angry or hurt by feedback from other people. Receiving positive and negative feedback is all part of a writers' workshop. Let Jane and me know when you feel hurt or angry, and we can talk about it, whether in the group or outside of the group."

"I agree," said Jane. "Having your writing critiqued by the group can sound like negative criticism. Your feelings can be hurt and you may feel angry. We are not here to hurt your feelings or make you feel angry. Try not to take the feedback personally. View the feedback a being helpful to you in becoming a better writer."

"However," said Sam, "there is a difference between giving feedback to the written work and being critical of an individual. To receive feedback we need to establish trust with one another and learn to accept feedback only on our written work, not personalities. Jane and I will not tolerate any critical statement about any person in this group. Are there any comments?"

"Very good," said Jane. "Now, let's begin to discuss the following tips. Let's start with 'who is your target audience?' " One by one the six participants began to share their target audience. Following the discussion it was time for lunch.

That evening around 7:00 the writers' group decided to have a beer at the Brew, a small pub on Spring Street. We decided to walk since we had been sitting all day. Sam and Jane decided not to go with us since they wanted to discuss the workshop. The women and the men walked separately to the Pub. Was it intentional or shyness? We have only known each other for a couple days and were hesitant about singling anyone out. At the pub we ordered beer and snacks. We shared our anxieties about the workshop and whether we could learn to write a murder mystery. Jokes were shared and we became more comfortable with each other. On the walk back to the house we mingled together, laughing and talking. When we arrived at the house everyone went to their room to write or go to sleep.

Sam and Jane were still working at the dining room table. Sam had produced a bottle of wine and they were drinking and laughing. Suddenly they heard the front door open. In walked Joanna, dressed casually in jeans and a t-shirt.

"Are you still working? I thought I might entice both of you to have a drink with me at Local Flavor, " she said.

"Go ahead;" said Jane, "I'm tired; I want to go to bed. I think my body is still on California time." Jane gathered books and papers and walked upstairs to her room.

Joanna turned to Sam, "Do you want to go to with me for a drink?"

"Thank you for asking, but I'm also tired. We have been to Local Flavor at least three times during the past couple of weeks. At another time, maybe we can go somewhere else," said Sam. He gave Joanna a hug and a kiss on the cheek and left the room.

Joanna felt hurt and rejected. "They had become so close during these past two weeks. Have his feelings changed towards her? Has Jane taken her place as a companion?" She was concerned. She drove home thinking about Sam. She realized that maybe she was mistaken in thinking that she and Sam had a relationship that was more than friendship. That night Joanna did not sleep well. She tossed and turned. Finally, she fell asleep around 1:00 a.m. after planning to confront Sam about their relationship.

Chapter Five

A week before the Murder Mystery workshop, Sam was enjoying the peace and quiet of the Writers' Colony. During the day he followed a schedule of writing. After breakfast, he wrote for three hours. After lunch, he took a walk and then continued writing from 2-5:00 p.m. In the evening Joanna joined him for dinner. They ate in the house or went out to eat. Local Flavor was Joanna's favorite place to eat. They became close friends. However, Sam's schedule changed at the beginning of the week before the Murder Mystery Workshop when Jane Foster Mason, Sam's co-instructor arrived.

Joanna had picked up Jane at the airport and drove directly to the Dairy Hollow House. As they talked on the way to Eureka Springs, Joanna became aware that there seemed to be a power struggle between the two women. Every time Joanna talked about a recent publication, Jane interrupted her and talked about her recent publication. Joanna soon stopped talking and let Jane talk. When they reached Dairy Hollow, Joanna was relieved. She introduced Jane to Helen, the registrar, and left the house. Helen showed Jane to her room.

After Jane unpacked, she walked down the stairs to meet with Sam at 10:00 a.m. As Jane walked down the stairs, she became aware of a familiar men's cologne, the same as a former lover. She saw Sam sitting at the dining room table drinking coffee. He was dressed casually in well-worn blue jeans and a white shirt. His dark hair looked windblown and there was a crumb of toast stuck in his beard.

"Good-morning, I am Jane Foster Mason. You must be Sam Peters," she said, and extended her hand to shake hands with Sam. Sam looked up from his writing and saw a tall, red haired woman with green eyes, wearing a black skirt with a green blouse. He pushed his chair aside, stood up, and shook her hand.

"I'm pleased to finally meet you," said Sam. "I read on Google all your accomplishments and the list of books and short stories that you have written. It is an honor to be working with you."

"I am so pleased to be asked to co-teach the Murder Mystery Workshop with you. Call me J.F., all my close friends do," said Jane. "This is the first time I've taught a class on writing a murder mystery. Have you taught before?"

"Yes, I have," said Sam, "at the local community college and several workshops. I brought a syllabus with me to show you what I have presented."

"What a relief," said Jane. "I thought we would have to start from a blank sheet of paper."

"Let me get you a cup of coffee. I am assuming you like it black?" asked Sam.

"Yes, I do."

Sam handed the syllabus to Jane and said, "You can read over the syllabus while I get the coffee."

"Good idea," said Jane.

After a few hours of talking and writing, they took a break. During the break they shared their interest in books.

"My first murder mystery books were Agatha Christie's," said Jane. "What were your first books?"

"I was a Sherlock Holmes fan. I've watched all the old and new movies and television shows of Sherlock Holmes. I prefer the British actors playing Sherlock and Watson."

"I like Sherlock Holmes' books as well. I also like Wilkie Collins' mysteries, *The Woman in White,* and *The Moonstone.* Have you read them?"

"Only recently," said Sam. "Those two books were

republished in 2003. Collins was a great writer. For light reading I enjoy books by David Baldacci and James Rollins."

"I agree," said Jane. "It seems we have favorite books in common. It's seems like we have known each other for a long time."

"Do you believe in past lives?" said Sam.

"Yes, living in California, it seems that almost everyone I know believes that we have had past lives or been reincarnated many times," said Jane.

"I agree," said Sam," maybe that can explain why we seem to have so much in common. I wonder if we shared some lives together."

Chapter Six

During the third morning session of the workshop, the members read the first chapters of their stories. Since Ted Simpson was from New Jersey, he wrote about a murder occurring on the Jersey Shore. Woody decided to write about the perfect murder. Sally Sanders, being a housewife, wrote about a murder in the suburbs. Gary Nelson, the Western writer from Little Rock, wrote about a cowboy committing a murder. Donna Rizman's murder was about an elderly man killed in a retirement village. My story featured a murder that was committed in an alleyway behind a bar. Jane and Sam provided helpful feedback on characterization and details. Around 11:30 the group broke for lunch.

Woody asked to see Sam out on the front porch. Both of them walked out of the house and sat on the porch. Since they left the door open, their conversation was easily overheard. "I'm really sorry for my behavior in the group," Woody said. "You have been so kind to me. I really appreciate it."

"Thank you," said Sam. "I enjoy having you in the group. You raise many good questions. You're off to a good start." Sam and Woody stood up and Sam gave Woody a hug. "Keep up the good work," said Sam. At lunch time Woody and Sam sat next to each other. They discussed various methods of how to murder a person. Other members of the group soon joined in.

That evening after dinner Woody said, "We men should go out for a drink. Sam, I want you to join us."

"Good idea," said the men. Sam hesitated and then said, "Yes, I'll go with you. Where do you want to go?"

"I am not sure, there are several options. Brews would be fun; they have a good selection of beers and ales," said Woody.

The men rode in Gary Nelson's car to Brews. They spent the evening drinking and talking.

I spent the evening in my room writing my murder mystery. I began to feel good about what I had written. Around 11:00 p.m. I heard the men open the front door. They were laughing and talking loudly. They sounded like college frat boys. I heard two men walk up the stairs to their rooms. The other two men must have stayed in the living room to talk. I fell asleep and awoke to a door closing down the hallway. My thought was that the two men downstairs were through talking and had gone to their rooms. I checked my cell phone and noticed that the time was midnight. I sighed and went back to sleep. The next morning, I overslept. I was going to be late for the workshop. I heard the group talking in the living room. But, I also heard someone crying. What was going on? I hurriedly ran down the stairs. To my surprise a Sheriff and Deputy were sitting at the dining room table talking to Ted and Gary. Sally Sanders was sitting in the living room crying. I walked over to her and sat down next to her.

"What happened? Are you okay?"

"Don't you know?" she said between tears. "Sam Peters, our instructor, was killed last night. The cook, Janice Henry, found his body in the kitchen lying in a pool of blood."

"Oh no, that is impossible!" I was shocked. I didn't know what to say. Finally, I said to her, "Where is the body now? Is it still in the kitchen?"

"The Sheriff told us, as a group, twenty minutes ago, that he was called around 6:15 a.m. because there was a dead man at the Writers' Colony. The Coroner took the body away at 7:00 a.m.," said Sally. "The Sheriff is interviewing each person to find out where they were last night."

"Does the Sheriff know how he was killed?" I asked her.

She replied, "He thought Sam was killed with a knife, but there was no weapon in sight."

We chatted for a while, and then I asked Donna, who was sitting on a chair near the fireplace, "How are you?"

"I guess I am as well as can be expected. Sam's death is such a tragedy. He was a good teacher. I will miss him."

We talked about him and the workshop and whether it would continue. After a while, I stood up and went to the dining room where a coffee pot was sitting on the buffet. I poured a cup and asked if Sue or Donna wanted any. They both said no. I drank the coffee and wandered around the room, not knowing what to do or say.

The Sheriff pushed his chair aside and stood up. He called the Deputy to come into the dining room. They talked for a few minutes, and then walked out of the house to their car.

I looked around at the workshop members and said, "Instead of waiting around the house, let's go to the kitchen and look around. Maybe the Deputy and Sheriff missed some clues."

"Who made you the leader?" sneered Ted.

"I just can't sit here and do nothing. If you don't want to help then sit there," I said in an impatient voice, "If anyone wants to go with me, let's go now."

As I walked to the kitchen, everyone followed me except Ted and Woody. Woody had gone to his bedroom, and Ted refused to help.

Each of us took a corner of the room. Gary took the south corner where the stove was. He looked at the top of the stove and then bent down to look under the oven.

"Look what I found under the stove!" he said with an excited voice as he was holding up a button, "Maybe it belongs to the murderer?"

"That's great," I said, "Let me get a Baggie and put the button in it. I'll give it to the Sheriff. Now, let's go outdoors and search the area to find anything else."

We walked outdoors and began searching the area. I noticed ashes in the patio fireplace. I found a stick and stirred the ashes. Most of the material was burned—the remains of papers and other trash. But underneath the ashes I found some torn papers that hadn't been completely burned. It was a hand-written note. I couldn't read all the writing, so I bagged it.

I said to the group, "Look what I found." I showed the torn pieces of paper to them and said, "I am going into the house and to my room to put the pieces together."

The group continued looking for the murder weapon and other clues. I walked into the house and up the stairs to my room. On the desk in my room, I laid out the burned pieces. It was like putting a puzzle together. I thought to myself, this is tedious. My fingers are getting black from the soot. After thirty minutes I had the pieces put together. I went to the bathroom to wash my hands and came back to read the note. As I read the note, I realized that it was a love note addressed to Sam. I read the note out loud.

"Dearest Sam,
I ....to be with .....please .... me.....
I love ..... Lets ...... some

Who wrote the note? I wondered. Shall I take this note to the Sheriff? Or, maybe it has nothing to do with Sam's murder. Since I'm a curious person, I decided to ask my fellow workshop members if they knew anyone in our writers' group in love with Sam. I left my room and walked downstairs. Sally had followed me into the house and was sitting in a chair. I sat down next to her.

"Sally, are you aware of anyone here at the workshop in love with Sam?"

"No, I don't think so. However, the interactions between Sam and Jane Foster seemed to demonstrate a close and warm relationship," said Sally.

"I agree," I said, "but maybe they are only good friends"

"Why are you asking?" said Sally. "Do you know something?"

"I don't know," I said. "I taped the pieces of paper together that I found outdoors in the fireplace. It was a love letter sent to Sam with no name of the person who sent it."

Sally asked, "Do you think it's a clue to who murdered Sam?"

"Maybe," I said.

The Sheriff had returned while I was upstairs in my room. He was sitting in a chair at the dining room table. He was talking to Joanna and Jane, who were sitting across from him. I couldn't help but overhear Joanna's loud voice saying that Jane was jealous of Joanna's relationship with Sam.

"No, I was not jealous of your relationship with Sam. We were just good friends," said Jane wiping her eyes with a tissue.

Joanna's voice seemed angry. I wondered if she felt threatened by Jane's close relationship with Sam. Then Joanna stormed angrily out of the house. I saw her drive away in her car.

"Can you show me Sam's room?" the Sheriff asked Jane.

"Yes, but first I want to use the restroom." Jane left the table to use the restroom on the second floor. Seeing that the Sheriff was alone, I approached him and said, "May I join you?"

"Certainly, sit down," said the Sheriff.

"I have several things to show you." I opened the baggie with the button inside. "Gary found this button in the kitchen. Do you think it is a clue to the murder?"

"Thank you, we must have missed it when we examined the kitchen," said the Sheriff.

"Also," I said, "I found this note outside in the fireplace. It was torn in pieces and partially burned." I gave the note to the Sheriff.

"Mmm, this note is interesting. It may have some bearing on the case. Thank you Sue, you have been most helpful. Is there anything else?"

"No," I said.

Jane came back into the room and beckoned the Sheriff to follow her upstairs. About thirty minutes later I saw the Sheriff returning to the dining room alone carrying a notebook. Did that notebook belong to Sam, I wondered. I wish I knew what was in it.

The Sheriff slipped the notebook and his other notes into his briefcase and left the house. As he was leaving, he said, "I'll be back."

After the Sheriff left I realized that it was lunch time. Joanna had sent Janice home to recover from the shock of finding a dead body in the kitchen. I was hungry, so were the other members of the workshop. None of us wanted to do any cooking.

Gary said, "I'll call a pizza delivery. We can all chip in."

We all agreed. When the pizza arrived 40 minutes later, we sat at the table and ate all of the three pizzas. There was little talking. The atmosphere seemed thick with sorrow.

At 1:00 p.m. Jane walked into the dining room and announced that we would meet. All members in the group left the table and joined Jane in the living room

Jane opened the session by saying, "The murder of Sam is a terrible thing to have happened. I think it would be best if each one of us shared how the murder of Sam is affecting us. We can support each other in our grief."

We spent the rest of the afternoon talking, crying, and trying to make some sense out of the murder. Joanna walked into the house and announced, "Janice, our cook, will not be preparing an evening meal tonight. There are salad materials in the refrigerator if you want to make your own dinner. Or, you can go out to a restaurant."

"Thanks, Joanna," said Jane. "Let's take the time now to discuss dinner plans."

While the group discussed what they wanted to do, Joanna and Jane walked to the office and began talking. I heard Joanna apologizing to Jane for her behavior earlier during the day. Jane responded by giving Joanna a hug and saying, "All of us admired and respected Sam. He was charming and easy to work with. There were no romantic feelings between us. I saw him more as a friend than a lover."

"Thank you for saying that," said Joanna. "I think I had developed romantic feelings towards him. I had hoped that he and I might become more than colleagues. I feel anger towards the murderer. Who could it have been?"

For dinner that evening all of the workshop members walked to Chelsea's restaurant. Joanna and Jane did not go with us; they had other plans. We sat outdoors since the temperature was in the 70s. When the waitress asked what we wanted to drink, I said, "I would like a glass of Merlot." Sally said, "I'll have a glass of Chablis." The others asked for a mixed drink or beer. We discussed Sam's murder, and who might have killed him.

After we ran out of theories, we began discussing our writings. Everyone had a unique story to share. We ordered more drinks and finally left the place around 8:30 p.m. We returned to the house by 9:00. All of us expressed how exhausted we were from the day's events. I was the first person to go to my room. I walked into the room, shut the door, and locked it. I did not want any surprises or visitors during the night, by the murderer, or anyone else, I thought to myself.

I'm not sure when the others went to their rooms; I was too tired to notice. I opened my notebook, and tried to write about the events of the day. I had a difficult time writing without tears splattering the paper.

Unbeknown to us, the Deputy had researched our backgrounds to see if any of us had a police record. Also, he checked our references to get personal statements about each of us. The Sheriff and the Deputy met all afternoon and evening to discuss the case, and narrowed the suspects down to two people.

Around 7:00 the next morning the Sheriff received a phone call telling him another murder had taken place at the Writers' Colony at Dairy Hollow. He called the Deputy and the Coroner to meet him there. They arrived at the house and were told that the body was upstairs in one of the bedrooms. Quickly they ran up the stairs

Chapter Seven

The sun was streaming through the window. I heard a wren singing; she might be gathering sticks and twigs to make a nest for her eggs. I guess it was time for me to get out of bed. I heard doors opening and closing, and footsteps running up and down the stairs. There was a lot of noise in the house this morning. I didn't want to get out of bed. I would rather be at home. Today is Thursday; maybe we could go home this afternoon. As I was getting dressed, I heard voices coming from downstairs. Quickly I ran down the stairs to see what was happening. As I looked around the room, I saw the Sheriff and the Deputy talking to Joanna in the office. Members of the Writers' Workshop were sitting at the dining room table drinking coffee except for Ted Simpson.

I walked over to the group and asked, "Where is Ted?"

Gary answered. "Ted has been murdered. I found him in his room. He didn't respond when I knocked on his door this morning. The door was not locked, so I walked in. I found him lying in bed with a pillow over him. What a shock! It's hard to believe! Immediately I called 911. The Sheriff, Deputy, and Coroner arrived 20 minutes later. The Sheriff said he was smothered by a pillow from his bed. They looked for fingerprints, but only found those of the victim."

"I pulled out a chair and sat down. I started crying. I noticed that Sue had moist red eyes, as did Donna. "I'm scared. Who's next?" I said. "What would be the motive?"

For the rest of the day the Sheriff interviewed each one of us in the office of the Writers' Colony house. Some of the questions he asked were: "Where were you between 10:00 p.m. and 8:00 a.m. this morning." Other questions were: "Did you like the victim? Did he like you? Did you know him before coming to this workshop? Did you have any augments with him?"

When it was my turn, I became very nervous.

I answered his questions by saying, "Ted wasn't well-liked. He had a loud voice, interrupted people when they were talking, and dominated the discussion. One time Ted and Woody got into an argument. Ted lacked empathy and social skills."

"Did anyone else get into an argument with Ted?" asked the sheriff.

"No, the rest of the group members were too polite to say anything to Ted. I sensed that people were angry with him, but they didn't speak up," I replied.

"Thank you, Miss Henry," said the Sheriff. "Who's next?" Donna stood up, and walked to the office to talk to the Sheriff.

I decided that I would try to figure out the identity of the murderer. I left the room, and walked upstairs to my room. I took out a sheet a paper, and put down the names of the four remaining workshop participants, as well as Jane and Joanna. That made six suspects; of course I eliminated myself. I tried to think who could be the murderer and what the motive might be. What would be gained from killing the victims? Who had a relationship with the victims? I drew a circle with Sam's name in the center. I drew two other circles around Sam's name. The circle that was close to Sam represented the people who had a relationship with him. In the second circle, I wrote the name of Joanna and Jane. In the third circle, I put the names of the people in the workshop.

It appeared that Joanna and Jane both had positive relationships with Sam. I didn't know if they had an intimate relationship with him or not. I do know that

Joanna was jealous of Jane's relationship with Sam. If Joanna was jealous of Jane, I would think that she would have killed Jane, not Sam. Unless, Sam favored Jane and rejected Joanna. Would Joanna be so angry that she killed Sam? And, I don't think Jane killed Sam. They seemed to work well together, and enjoyed each other's company. They were colleagues, maybe lovers? I wondered.

I looked at the names of the workshop participants. Did any of them have a motive? Did anyone dislike Sam? It was difficult for me to think that one of the group members killed Sam. All of us got along so well, except for Ted; no one seemed to like him. However, Sam and Jane accepted Ted as a member, and tried to be positive towards him.

The more I thought, the more confused I became. After so much thinking, I began to get a headache. I decided to stop working and go downstairs to join the others. I walked to the kitchen and poured a cup of coffee. I joined some of the group members sitting at the dining room table.

After everyone had been interviewed, the Sheriff said, "I will return at 1:00 p.m. to meet with the whole group. I hope to have some questions answered. No one can leave this house—you are all suspects."

After the Sheriff left, we all looked at one another, wondering who the murderer was. I sat close to Donna and Sally. We were scared. Were we safe? I did not think that a woman was the murderer. We sat on the couch, drinking coffee and talking in low voices, until the Sheriff returned

Chapter Eight

The tension in the Writers' Colony at Dairy Hollow was felt by all the participants in the Writers' Workshop. There was a lot of coffee and tea drinking by the participants, possibly even a little alcohol in a cup. At 12:45 all of us, including Jane and Joanna, gathered in the living room. We spoke in low voices to each other, wondering what the Sheriff wanted to say. At 1:00 the Sheriff and his Deputy arrived. The Deputy stayed by the front door while the Sheriff took a chair near the entrance of the living room.

He said, "Thank you for attending this meeting. I have discovered that one of you is the murderer."

Everyone started talking at once and looking at each other.

"Quiet, please. Let me state the evidence. We couldn't find the murder weapon at first. Then my Deputy used an infrared wand in all the drawers in the kitchen. One of the large kitchen knives had blood stains. We took it back to the lab to find fingerprints, but they were washed off. Whoever stabbed the victim must have had blood on his or her shirt. When we searched the house, we found the shirt, with blood stains and a button missing, at the bottom of a clothes hamper in the laundry room. The shirt was made for an extra-tall man or woman. The missing button that Miss Sue gave me matched the buttons on the bloodstained shirt. Our third clue was a torn love note written to the murder victim. Someone in this room was in love with the victim. All of you fell under suspicion. My Deputy made a search of all your backgrounds, and we narrowed the suspects down to the individuals who are not married or in a relationship. In the beginning I suspected that the love letter had been written by either Jane or Joanna, since Joanna expressed jealousy of Jane's relationship with the victim. It turned out that both of them were not in the house the night of the first murder. Joanna was at home, and her housemate vouched for her. Jane had an alibi since she spent the night at the Crescent Hotel. The people at the Crescent Hotel desk saw her check in."

"I heard that the Crescent Hotel was haunted," said Jane. "I wanted to have an experience of a ghostly visitor. I stayed in a room which was supposed to be haunted. By morning I had not seen a ghost. I was disappointed. I didn't tell anyone that I had left. I had hoped to have a story to tell all of you."

"Since the two women had alibis that left us with one other individual. However, we lacked the motive," said the Sheriff. "The final clue was the victim's notebook. In the notebook was a diary. The diary was started three years ago at a writers' workshop in Iowa. The victim had written of a relationship he had had with a workshop participant. He had called it off at the end of the workshop and never mentioned that person again. Also, he wrote about his wife and her anger when she found out that he had sexual affairs outside the marriage. She subsequently divorced him, and he was devastated by the divorce.

He came to Arkansas to attempt to put his life back together. It was at this present writers' workshop that he met the person he had an affair with three years ago. The person's name and hair had been changed. By putting all the facts together, the murderer is," . . . He turned to look at the group and paused. Then he looked at the men and pointed to Woody and said, "Woody Wilson, although that is not your birth name, you are the murderer."

"No, wait a minute, it was an accident. I was in love with Sam; I wrote the note hoping to rekindle our relationship. At first, he hadn't recognized me since I had shaved my beard, dyed my hair, and changed my name. When the men all went out together for a beer, he recognized me, but didn't say anything in front of the other men. After we walked back to the house, Gary and Ted went upstairs to bed. Sam and I went into the kitchen to talk. Sam was angry. He confronted me by saying, "Why are you here? I called off the relationship three years ago."

"I told him that I couldn't forget him, that I loved him. As I leaned over to kiss him, Sam backed away and swung his fist at me. I felt so rejected and angry that I fought back. I knocked him down, and he swore at me. I was enraged. I grabbed a knife from the drawer and plunged it into his chest. I didn't mean to kill him. It was an accident. I loved him," he sobbed. "I loved him."

"What about the second murder," asked the Sheriff? "Why did you kill Ted?

"I had to kill Ted. He had walked downstairs to get a drink from the kitchen and overheard Sam and me talking. The next day he said he would tell the Sheriff what he heard. To keep him from talking, I would have to pay him fifty thousand dollars. I didn't have that kind of money; I had no other option but to kill him."

"Deputy, come here and cuff the man and take him to jail," said the Sheriff. The Deputy walked over to Woody, cuffed him, and took him out of the house to the police car. All of us were stunned. We look at each other and just shook our heads. "It can't be true," murmured various members.

The Sheriff told us that we were free to go home. We four remaining workshop members left the room and went upstairs to pack. After we had packed our clothes and books, we gathered in the living room to say our good-byes. We hugged each other and promised to keep in touch. Silently we walked to our cars and drove away.

Epilogue

A year has gone by since the Murder Mystery Workshop occurred at the Dairy Hollow Writers' Colony. Finally, I was able to gain some objectivity concerning the two murders. I wrote this story from the notes that I took at the workshop. Even today I am not sure how objective I was. I realized that the murder mystery turned out to be a love story, a crime of passion.

I have kept in touch with the other participants in the Murder Mystery Writers' workshop. Many of them have tried to write a murder mystery; only two succeeded, Donna Rizman and Gary Nelson. Gary combined a murder mystery story with his favorite genre, the western. Donna's story was a murder in a retirement village.

She said, "I rewrote the story and turned it into a play. The play was performed in a community room at a local village for retired people. I received many compliments for the play."

Will I write another murder mystery, I thought to myself? Yes, to that question, but only from my own imagination. I do not wish to have another firsthand experience in a murder mystery, as I did in Eureka Springs.

Characters

Joanna Reeves, Executive Director of the Writers Colony

Sheriff, Carroll County

Deputy, Carroll County

Coroner, Carroll County

Helen, Registrar, Eureka Springs

Jane Foster Mason, Instructor of the Workshop, Professional writer for 20 years, lives in California

Writers Attending the Workshop

Ted Simpson, banker from New Jersey

Woody Wilson, writer from Iowa

Sally Sanders, housewife from Rogers, AR

Gary Nelson, businessman from Little Rock

Donna Rizman, retired, from Ok

Sue Henry, writer, Springfield, MO.

Janice Henry, the cook, Eureka Springs

Sam Peters, writer-in-residence, professional writer, lives in the Chicago suburbs, has published a murder mystery novel and several short stories.

MURDER AT THE CRESCENT HOTEL

Dedication

This book is dedicated to all the people who like a good mystery/ghost story set in a Victorian hotel.

Thanks to Don Soderberg for encouraging me to wrie.

Introduction

The setting for this story is the Crescent Hotel, located in Eureka Springs, in the Ozark Mountain region of Northwest Arkansas. Between 1884 and 1886 the hotel was built on the crest of West Mountain. Eureka Springs was noted for its healing springs. During the late 1800s, people traveled from all over the country to take in the waters and cure their ailments. Spring water could also be bottled and shipped out to all parts of the country.

In 1908 the hotel was opened as the Crescent College and Conservatory for Young Women, and served as an exclusive academy for wealthy ladies. Due to the high costs of running the school, it was closed in 1924. It reopened briefly from 1930 to 1934 as a junior college. After the college closed, the Crescent was leased for a short time as a summer hotel.

Then in 1937 Norman Baker leased the hotel to turn it into a hospital and health resort. Norman Baker saw himself as a medical expert. He claimed to have discovered a number of cures for various ailments. In 1940 he was charged by the federal authorities with using the mail to defraud the public with his false medical claims, and he was sentenced to four years in Leavenworth. The hotel was closed until 1946. New investors purchased the hotel in 1997 and began to restore it. The owners oversaw a six-year restoration and renovation of the hotel rooms.

Called "America's Most Haunted Hotel," it is said to be haunted by at least eight spirits. ESP weekend, held each year for three days in January, features an expertly guided, behind the scenes quest for evidence of spirits in the hotel.

Chapter One

Myrtle had worked as a maid at the Crescent Hotel for the past fifteen years. She was considered an 'old timer' by the other maids. Also, she was one of the few maids to clean the haunted rooms that are listed in the hotel's brochures. The other maids were too scared to go near those rooms. Myrtle scoffed at their fears; she knew better.

"It's just a publicity stunt to get guests to stay at this old hotel," she said to her husband when he asked her if she was afraid of the ghosts.

She enjoyed working at the hotel and felt proud of her work which was praised by the manager. But this morning Myrtle did not want to go to work. She wanted to attend the morning services at St. Elizabeth's where her niece's baby was to be baptized.

But, it was her scheduled weekend to work. She didn't have to be there until 9:00 a.m. Most of the guests didn't check out until 11:00 a.m.; but she liked to get to the hotel early and do all the preparations for cleaning the rooms. She usually arrived at 8:45 a.m.; it gave her extra time to head to the laundry room and gather all her linens.

In the laundry room, she saw Rachel Beth taking linens from the dryer. Rachel Beth was one of her best friends. Often, they took breaks together and went for smoke breaks outside the building.

As Myrtle walked toward the laundry room, she noticed that a door to a closet in the hallway was left ajar. That door is supposed to be locked, she thought. She walked over to the door and noticed a shoe blocking it. As she squeezed through the doorway, she saw a body attached to the shoe.

She was horrified at the sight—a body and a bloody head. She began screaming and fled the room yelling, "Help! Help!"

Hearing her cries, Rachel Beth rushed to Myrtle's side.

"What happened? Are you hurt? Did you see a ghost?"

"There's a body in that room! He looks dead! Call the police!"

Immediately, Rachel Beth took out her cell phone and called the front desk.

In a shaky and anxious voice she said, "There's a dead body in the basement."

Bill, a young man working at the front desk answered the call. "What did you say? Repeat your message. Did you say a body is in the basement? Yes, I hear you!"

He hung up, immediately called 911, and gave them the message. Although there were several people waiting to check out, he asked them to wait.

"Please excuse me. I need to talk to my manager."

Then he ran to the business office and shared with the manager what had just happened. The manager quickly ran down the stairs to the basement. He saw Myrtle and Rachel Beth huddled in a corner of the washroom with their arms around each other.

"Where's the body?" he said.

They pointed to the open closet door in the hallway. The manager walked over to the room and stepped inside. He saw a man with a bloody head. Clearly, the man was dead. The manager felt sick to his stomach and left the room. He walked back up the stairs to wait for the Sheriff to arrive.

Within the next twenty minutes, the Sheriff and his Deputy arrived in the Sheriff's car and parked in the circle drive of the hotel. Following close behind was the van of the Coroner and his staff.

Seeing the Sheriff's car, the manager rushed out the front door to greet him.

"Hello, Sheriff. Follow me," said the manager.

The Sheriff, Deputy, and Coroner followed the manager down the service stairway to the basement. The manager pointed to the open closet door. The room was too small for more than one person to enter. The Sheriff took one look and stepped aside for the Coroner to check out the body.

After about ten minutes, the coroner came out of the room and said, "That man was shot in the head. His knuckles are bruised and there's skin under his nails. I have to take the body to the morgue and do an autopsy."

"Go right ahead," said the Sheriff. "I'll send my Deputy upstairs and ask my staff to come down here and remove the body."

"Thanks. That'll save me from running up and down those stairs. I'm not as young as I use to be; I like my fried chicken and mashed potatoes a little too much, I guess."

"Can you identify this man?" asked the Sheriff looking at the manager.

"I don't know. Maybe he's a guest. I'll have to check with the front desk." The manager then walked upstairs to talk to the staff.

The Coroner took the body to the morgue to do the autopsy. The Sheriff followed the manager up the stairs and sat on one of the couches in the lounge area, curious to find out if the dead man was a registered guest.

Chapter Two

On a hot, muggy July morning, Jason Pierson walked to work; that is, he assumed the identity of a homeless person and walked to the city park and mingled with other homeless people. Jason is thirty-five years old, single, and a police officer who has worked for the Memphis Police Department for the past ten years. He had a six month old beard and wore a torn knit hat over long, dirty brown hair. He called himself "Hal." A year ago, he was involved in a bitter divorce. To keep his anger in check, he asked to be assigned as an undercover police officer. He needed a change of pace, something different than sitting in an office. A drug ring was discovered in Memphis, and Jason was assigned to search for the ringleaders even though he had no prior experience.

He was coached by Jackie, another undercover police officer, in what to wear and how to act. Jackie, a young

African-American woman, dressed like a street person. She wore dirty slacks, a turtleneck sweater, and a coat with torn pockets and moth holes. Jason bought his clothes at Goodwill. He had picked out the most threadbare trousers with holes in the knees. He wore a dirty t-shirt, a flannel shirt, and an old denim jacket. At night he slept in a homeless shelter and ate his meals at the Salvation Army. Once a week he and Jackie met at a nearby coffee shop to compare notes. Over the new few weeks, they also became good friends. Jason was able to confide in her the story of his divorce and former wife. In turn, she shared her story of her fiancé, an army sergeant who was killed in Afghanistan.

During one of their weekly meetings, Jackie gave him the name of a drug dealer, Nate Mills, and his contact information. Jason was assigned to make friends with Nate and find out the name of Nate's boss. Jason followed the lead and met Nate in a local bar. Jason became Nate's customer, buying drugs on a weekly basis. Every week Jason turned the drugs into police headquarters. After a month had gone by, Jason asked Nate, "How can I become a dealer. I really need the money."

Nate replied, "I like you, Hal; I'll ask my boss if you can become a dealer. I'll get back to you tomorrow around noon. Let's meet in the park by the Andrew Jackson statue, one of the founders of Memphis."

The next day around noon, Jason and Nate met near the statue in the park. "Well, Nate, do you have good news for me?" asked Jason.

"Yeah, I talked to my boss, Carlos. He wants to meet you. There's an opening for a dealer. The man who had that job left for Chicago. You can become a dealer, but you need to dress like one. Here's a hundred dollars. Use it to buy some new clothes. You can pay me back after your first paycheck. Also, trim your beard and take a bath. We'll meet Carlos at his favorite bar, the one he goes to every evening. Meet me here tomorrow night at 9:00—and Jason, wear your new clothes."

"Thanks," said Jason, "I'll see you tomorrow evening." Jason walked a few blocks and stopped in the doorway of a bookstore. He took out his phone and called Jackie. "Can you meet me at our usual time and place today?"

"Yes," said Jackie, "I'll be there in a couple hours."

Jason put his phone in his pocket and walked to the nearest department store. With the hundred dollars that Nate had given him, Jason purchased a pair of jeans, a white shirt, and t-shirt. He found a nice looking wool jacket at Goodwill. With the few dollars he had left, he walked to a drug store to purchase a razor and shaving cream. Then he walked to the meeting place, ordered coffee, and waited for Jackie.

When Jackie arrived, she was pleased to see him and hear the good news about the meeting that was set up with the drug boss, Carlos.

Jackie was dressed as a homeless person. She had a shopping cart filled with bags of stuff.

"I'm so glad to hear the good news. I'm sure you'll be accepted. If you meet this guy and find a way for us to arrest him, we'll have to celebrate," she said.

"What do you have in mind?" Jason responded in a teasing voice.

"I'll leave it to your imagination. But, now, we need to plan your strategy for meeting Carlos."

For the next hour Jackie and Jason planned several scenarios. When they decided on one, they left the café and went their separate ways.

The next evening Nate drove his car to the park and picked up Jason. Nate drove to a bar on the south side of town. They walked into the bar and looked around for Carlos. Carlos and one of his bodyguards were sitting in a booth at the end of the room. Carlos was wearing a navy blue suit, white shirt, and a gold cross on a chain around his neck. Nate and Jason walked to the booth and sat opposite Carlos. Nate introduced Jason to Carlos.

"Carlos, I want you to meet a friend of mine; his name is

Hal. He's interested in becoming a dealer."

Carlos reached across the table with his right hand and shook hands with Jason.

"I'm glad to meet you, Hal. We can use another dealer for the northwest side of the city. Have you ever sold drugs before, in this city or elsewhere?"

"I did a little when I lived in Cincinnati. But I started using the drugs and almost overdosed one night. I was sent to a rehab center for six weeks. Then I moved to Memphis."

"I don't like my dealers doing drugs; it eats into the profits," said Carlos.

"Sounds good to me. How do I get started?"

"Nate seems to like you and will vouch for you as being trustworthy. Before I make a decision, I will check my horoscope for tomorrow to see if it is a good day to make a decision. Nate will let you know whether I accept you or not. It's all up to the stars to help me make that decision. If you are accepted, you can attend a meeting with us tomorrow evening."

The next day Jason received a call from Nate.

"Carlos has accepted you. Congratulations. He said that his horoscope for the day was, 'A new person will be joining his business.' Carlos is very superstitious. He doesn't do anything without checking his daily horoscope. Meet me at the park at our usual place, 45 minutes after midnight. I will take you to the meeting, which will be at the waterfront, warehouse number 4."

"Sounds good to me. I'll be there at 12:45."

Jason was so excited. Finally, he caught a break. They might be able to arrest Carlos and other dealers. He called Jackie and told her the good news. She called her captain and arranged for a police squad to come to the warehouse around 1:10.

The next evening Jason met Nate at 12:45 in the park. Nate drove them to the warehouse to meet with the drug ring. Carlos was the only ringleader present. Jason observed that there were four men. He assumed they were drug dealers talking to Carlos. Carlos greeted Nate and Jason and introduced Jason to the other drug dealers.

At ten minutes after 1:00, the group was interrupted by a loud voice, "Police! You're under arrest!"

The drug dealers pulled out their guns and began shooting in the direction of the voice. Carlos, at the police warning, quickly slipped through a trap door which led to the waterfront. Jason pulled out his gun, and followed Carlos through the trap door. Carlos turned around and shot Jason in the shoulder. Jason fell down holding his hand over the wound. The captain followed Jason through the trapdoor and saw that Jason was bleeding.

"It looks like you've been shot. I'll call for help."

An ambulance arrived ten minutes later. Jason was rushed to the nearest hospital and taken to the emergency room. He was treated, moved to a room, and kept overnight.

Fortunately, the bullet didn't go through any bones or arteries. Jason felt lucky. The next day he was sent home to rest and heal. Jackie visited Jason on a daily basis. Often she brought food and drinks.

After two months of rest and rehab, Jason went back to work at a desk in the police headquarters. His shoulder was tender, and he knew he would be useless in a fight. Also, since his cover was blown, he could no longer be an uncover cop. He felt disappointed. He didn't like his desk job.

At the end of November, Jason received some information about Carlos. He had either moved to Chicago or St. Louis. The captain assigned the case to Jason. Jason was no longer bored. He felt the excitement of the chase growing within him. First, he asked the artist at police headquarters to draw a portrait of Carlos from the description he gave them. The portrait was e-mailed to police departments in St. Louis and Chicago. Within a couple of weeks Jason received a notice from a precinct in St. Louis that they may have seen Carlos. The next day Jason drove to St. Louis to follow the lead.

After arriving in St. Louis, Jason immediately drove to the precinct where Carlos had been spotted. He met with Bill Haley, Chief of Detectives.

"Can you give me any information about Carlos?" Jason asked Detective Haley.

Haley responded, "Carlos was seen in a bar with a young woman. Around his neck he wore a gold chain with a gold cross."

"Do you have an address for the bar?" Jason asked.

"Yes, I have the address written down." He picked up a card off his desk and gave it to Jason.

"Thanks. If you receive any more information, please call me." Jason gave his cell phone number to Detective Haley and said, "See you later." He shook hands with Detective Haley and left the precinct. Wasting no time, Jason drove to the bar. He walked inside the building and showed the man behind the bar his police badge and a photo of Carlos. "Have you seen this man?"

"Yeah, he was a regular for a few weeks, and then he stopped coming in. Often he came in with a blonde woman. The woman called him Arnold, and he called her Sandy. The last time they were in here, they were sitting at the bar holding hands and drinking beer. Arnold put down his beer and took out his wallet. He showed the woman several hundred dollar bills and said he had enough money to take them on a trip. The woman laughed. She said that she had made plans to spend a weekend in Eureka Springs in January, attending an ESP workshop at a historic hotel called the Crescent where ghosts have been seen. She said that he should come with her.

"Before Arnold could agree to the trip, they were interrupted by a loud drunk who made a pass at Sandy. Arnold told the man to leave. The man ignored him. Arnold pulled out a gun and told the man he would shoot him if he didn't leave. The man raised his hands and said, 'I'm leaving.' I told Arnold that guns were not permitted in here. He would have to leave, or I would call the police."

"Did they say anything else?" Jason asked.

"No, but Arnold was mad; he swore at me, and told me to watch my back. When they left, I called the police and reported the incident."

"Thanks for the information; I'll follow that lead."

Jason left St. Louis and drove back to Memphis. On the drive back he called Jackie and told her what had happened.

"I plan to attend that ESP workshop in Eureka Springs in hopes of finding Carlos. If you can get away, would you come with me in disguise? We could be a couple from Jonesboro."

She said, "That sounds like fun, as well as dangerous."

"When I arrive at headquarters, I'll talk to the captain. See you soon."

On his arrival at police headquarters, he knocked on the door of the Captain's office. The Captain opened his door and said, "Welcome back. Did you gain any new information about Carlos?"

"Yes, as a matter of fact, I gained a great deal of information." He shared all the information that he had learned. "I want to catch Carlos and bring him in. When I follow Carlos to Eureka Springs I'll need a disguise. I would like Jackie to accompany me—we could go as a couple.

The Captain said, "I'll think about it. I'll give you my answer tomorrow. Go home and rest. You've been doing a lot of driving."

Jason left the building and drove to his apartment. He didn't bother taking off his clothes or shoes; he flopped on the bed and immediately fell asleep.

Chapter Three

Although the snow was blowing and the temperature was in the 20s on this January day in Eureka Springs, Fred Von Briesen, the program director of the ESP Weekend at the Crescent Hotel, looked forward to the third ESP workshop. He had been hired four years before to be the guide for the weekend tours of the haunted Crescent Hotel. Born in West Germany in 1948, his parents left Germany when he was three years old and settled in New York City. His father became a shoe store manager, and his mother worked as an elementary school teacher. He was raised in a northern suburb of New York City and attended a private school.

At an early age he discovered that he enjoyed making people laugh. In high school he joined the drama club and found an outlet for his need for attention. On weekends he auditioned for parts in plays produced by the local theater group. Gradually he became a regular cast member. After high school, he attended a city college and majored in theater and speech. He became a popular star in the college plays, because he took on the roles of villains and was very convincing.

After college Fred worked at odd jobs, and played bit parts in Off-Broadway shows for the next twenty years. He married one of the actresses, Ginger Lane. They met when they were both cast in a play. They spent many happy years together. During the month of April, when Fred turned fifty-one, he had a heart attack, retired from acting, and stayed home. But because he was no longer able to be an actor, he felt depressed.

"I don't know what to do. Is my life over?" said Fred.

Ginger replied, "I think you need to consult with your physician about your emotional state."

"That sounds like a good idea," said Fred.

After a visit with his physician, he was told that it was normal for him to feel depressed after a heart attack. The physician gave Fred a prescription for an anti-depressant. The anti-depressant helped for a while, but Fred was still wondering what to do with life. He felt useless and bored.

Several months later Ginger said, "Why don't we have a change of scenery. Let's take a vacation to the South during the month of September or October. Most people will have already taken their vacations and will be back at work."

Fred replied, "That sounds like a good idea."

They decided to get some information from a travel agent. The agent showed them pamphlets of places to visit in the South. The colorful pamphlets of Asheville, North Carolina and Eureka Springs, Arkansas looked inviting. The temperature in late September and early October would still be warm. The colors of the fall would be beautiful then. They took the literature home with them, and discussed the pros and cons of each place. Because Eureka Springs was designated a historical village with intact Victorian homes and hotels, they felt drawn there; and after looking at the various places to stay, they chose the Crescent Hotel. They made plans to spend a week in Eureka Springs.

Ginger made reservations for the plane trip to Northwest Arkansas and the hotel stay at the Crescent Hotel for the second week in October.

When they arrived at the airport, they rented a car and on their arrival in Eureka Springs were in awe of the colorful beauty of the Ozark hills and all the Victorian homes and storefronts.

Ginger said, "I feel like we have stepped back in time, maybe a hundred years ago."

They drove through the city, up Spring Street, until they

arrived at the Crescent Hotel.

"What a beautiful and well preserved hotel," said Fred. As they checked into the hotel and their room,

"We have made a good choice. I am anxious to explore the village and visit the shops," Ginger said.

After resting for a couple hours, Sam and Ginger drove down to Main Street and parked next to the Eureka Springs Historical Museum. They noticed the colorful gardens on both sides of the building. Inside the museum, they saw a woman at the counter.

She said, "Welcome to the Eureka Springs Historical Museum. The fee is $5.00 per person."

Fred paid her with a $10.00 bill. She said, "Thank you. This museum is a non-profit institution whose primary purpose is the collecting, preserving, documenting, and exhibiting physical objects of historical significance. Eureka Springs is a town which grew up from the discovery of a spring of healing waters during the last two decades of the nineteenth century. It was built on a seemingly inexhaustible supply of pure, clear water that healed; it became a health spa, and was the fourth largest city in Arkansas from 1879 to the turn of the century. This building originally had living quarters on the second floor, and a store on the first floor. It was called the Calif Building in 1889. You may walk around the museum on the first floor and then walk upstairs to the art collection on the second floor. At the end of your tour, you may stop in our gift shop and look at all the books that have been published about Eureka Springs.

After their tour of the museum, Fred and Ginger began walking down the streets and looking inside all the storefronts. They saw a coffee shop on Spring Street and decided to rest for a while and drink coffee. The coffee shop had its original tin ceiling that was at least 15 to 20 feet high. Because of the height of the ceiling, the small coffee shop seemed larger than it really was.

After they drank their coffee, they decided to walk back to their car and were grateful that the walk was downhill.

For the next few days Fred and Ginger toured Eureka Springs and the surrounding area. One day they drove to Beaver Lake and took a boat ride to see the eagles. Another day they drove east to visit one of the many caves in Arkansas.

When they were ready to leave, Ginger said, "What a charming place to live. Why don't we consider moving here?"

"I agree; but first, let's go home and think about it" said Fred.

They went home, thought about it, and moved to Eureka Springs six months later. They found a small three bedroom cottage on Prospect Street in Eureka Springs. After spending a month decorating the cottage, they began enjoying retirement. But three months later, Fred was feeling bored.

"I want to get a job. I am bored with retirement. I don't know what to do without having a job."

"You can't be serious," said Ginger.

"Yes, I am. I'm going to look for a job," said Fred. He picked up the weekly Eureka Springs paper. At the back of the newspaper, he found the want ads. He found an ad for a part-time person to give talks and lead tours at the Crescent Hotel.

"Ginger, look what's in the newspaper? There's a part-time job at the Crescent Hotel. I'm going to apply for it."

Fred was hired and began working there on a part-time basis. Three years later he was still working at the Crescent. One day, he had a great idea. Why not have an ESP workshop at the Crescent Hotel to coincide with the UFO Conference? The manager of the hotel approved of the idea and asked Fred to organize the workshop and be the facilitator. He had his choice of speakers and a budget to pay for them. In January he held a weekend ESP workshop. It proved to be a very successful event. The second year the workshop had more participants than the previous year.

For the third workshop he hired a couple from Colorado. He was excited about having new speakers for the event.

Chapter Four

In spite of the blowing snow and cold temperature, Donna Jewett and Jerry Weisfeld arrived by United Airlines at XNA airport in Bentonville, Arkansas from Denver, Colorado on Sunday afternoon, January 5. Donna was a tall middle-aged woman with bleached blonde hair and blue eyes, wearing a gray wool suit and white blouse. Jerry was ten years younger. His hair was black, and he had dark brown eyes. He wore blue jeans, a red shirt, and a dark corduroy jacket. They had been married for twenty years. They met when she was teaching a class at the local university, and he was a student in her class. After a two year relationship they decided to get married.

They were excited about coming to Arkansas for the first time to be speakers at the ESP workshop at the Crescent Hotel in Eureka Springs. They were invited to speak since they had published a book, *Discovering Ghosts in Colorado Ghost Towns.*

After picking up their checked bags, Jerry walked to the car rental office while Donna stopped at the coffee shop for an espresso. Jerry was given the keys to a Ford SUV. They walked to the rental car lot and found their car. Jerry put in the suitcases in the trunk, while Donna slid into the driver's seat.

"I thought I was going to drive," said Jerry.

"No, I want to drive. You look at the map and tell me how to get to Eureka Springs," said Donna.

"Okay, but I would prefer to drive. The roads can be icy; be careful," said Jerry.

"You know that I get carsick when we drive through mountains," said Donna.

Jerry nodded his head and looked at the directions that were given to him when he rented the car. Also, he looked at the map to get a better overall perspective of the state. As Donna drove away from the airport, Jerry directed her to head toward the interstate and take Highway 62 to Eureka Springs. Donna turned on the radio, which led to very little conversation between the two. Occasionally she'd make a comment about the curves or the beautiful vistas. Jerry merely grunted.

On their arrival in Eureka Springs, they stopped at Myrtie Mae's for a late lunch. Both of them ordered the salad bar with soup. After lunch, Donna followed the directions to the Crescent Hotel by taking Spring Street to Prospect. When they turned the corner and viewed the Crescent Hotel, both of them paused.

Donna said, "What a beauty! She's larger than the photos. I'm impressed."

She parked the SUV in the hotel's parking lot. The snow had been removed, and salt had been spread on the sidewalk and steps of the hotel to prevent any guests from slipping on the ice. They removed their luggage from the trunk, and Donna locked the car. As they walked up the steps to the hotel lobby, the massive door was opened by a young doorman.

"Welcome to the Crescent Hotel." Both Donna and Jerry said, "Thank you."

Immediately Donna walked to the reception desk to register. She was given the keys to their room which was on the second floor. The couple walked upstairs to their room, followed by the young doorman who was carrying their luggage. Donna opened the door with one of the room keys. The room was large with two double beds, a desk, and a large window which overlooked the cold, wintery garden. Donna tipped the doorman and closed the door.

Jerry said, "What a relief! I'm tired. I'm going to take a nap."

He took off his shoes, flopped on one of the beds, and was soon sleeping and snoring. Donna shook her head with a disgusted look on her face and opened her purse. She took out a small bottle of wine and poured it into a glass. She slowly sipped the wine and studied the workshop schedule. She and her husband would be speaking on Saturday afternoon. She was listed as a psychic who helped ghosts head towards the light. Jerry was listed as an investigator of ghosts. She thought I hope Jerry is prepared; I know I am.

For dinner that evening they chose to eat in the Crystal Ball Room at the hotel. Jerry ordered steak, salad, and a glass of Merlot; Donna ordered fish.

"I hope you're prepared for our presentation Saturday afternoon," Donna said.

"Don't worry! I'm prepared, and I have the next few days to review my notes. Let's plan to take a tour of the hotel so we can get a sense of what kind of ghosts we might encounter."

"That's a good idea," said Donna. "I certainly don't wish to participate in any kind of hoax."

"You never know," said Jerry. "But, the written account of the history of ghosts in this hotel is intriguing. I am curious. I hope my equipment can pick up any evidence of ghosts."

Their meal was delicious. Following dinner they decided to have dessert. Donna chose a cheesecake and Jerry chose a chocolate cake. They both ordered decaf coffee with cream. Following dinner they left the Crystal Ball Room and walked to the sitting room in front of the fireplace. The warm fire felt good on this cold January evening.

Chapter Five

On a sunny, clear day in January I drove to Eureka Springs from my home in Springfield, Missouri. On the way I stopped by my friend Anna Marie's house to pick her up. As I stopped in front of her house, she walked down the steps carrying a large suitcase. I stepped out of the car to open the trunk and said, "Hi, Anna Marie, are you ready for the trip?"

"Hi, Sue. Yes, I'm ready. I've been looking forward to this workshop for a long time."

I lifted the heavy suitcase, with help from Anna Marie, and we put it in the trunk next to my suitcase. I closed the trunk and walked around the car to the driver's door. I was wearing my new jeans and a jean jacket. Ann Marie was also wearing jeans and a red wool jacket sweater. She opened the door to the passenger side and sat down, closing the door.

We met at a writers' group in Springfield a year ago. Both of us were middle-aged women, married, with kids in college. I'm a mystery writer, and Anna Marie is a writer of ghost and murder mysteries. Anna Marie had checked online to find the nearest haunted mansions that she could visit. She wanted to spend a night in a haunted mansion and write a story about her experiences. On the internet, she found a three day ESP Weekend held every year in January at the Crescent Hotel in Eureka Springs, Arkansas. She convinced me to go with her and share a room. I searched the Crescent Hotel web page, and found the following information:

Perched high above the Victorian village of Eureka Springs, Arkansas – recognized by the National Trust for Historic Preservation as one of America's Dozen Distinctive Destinations – is the 1886 Crescent Hotel & Spa, a palatial structure and landmark hotel known widely as the 'symbol of hospitality' for the State of Arkansas and Ozark Mountain region. . .

The Crescent has retained its 19th Century Character: the 14-foot ceilings of the Crystal Ballroom, the elegant and hand-painted lobby, the upscale guest rooms, and the large verandas that allow guests to enjoy the fresh mountain air.

What an impressive description of an old hotel! I wondered what Eureka Springs is like. I continued reading:

The Crescent Hotel is located in the Eureka Springs Historic District – home to more than 100 restored Victorian shops, restaurants, and art galleries, surrounded by hundreds of Victorian cottages, ample green space, and walking trails that connect the tower of native limestone to the Downtown District.

The Crescent Hotel and Eureka Springs sounded like a great place to visit and a step back in time to the Victorian period. In November we sent in reservations for the hotel and the special event. For the next two months I conducted research on haunted mansions and ghosts. I wanted to be prepared for the ESP Weekend. Also, I began watching, 'Ghost Hunters' on the SyFy television channel. As I watched, I began laughing at the absurdity of it. The show seemed to have little content or results of their investigations. I didn't share my feelings and thoughts with Anna Marie about the television show. I didn't want to spoil her experiences at the Crescent Hotel.

The drive seemed long due to having to slow down as we drove on the icy hills and valleys. I was taking the shortcut to Eureka Springs. As we drove across the bridge over Table Rock Lake, I noticed the sun reflecting off the water, creating a shimmering effect. It seemed like a magic moment. When we drove over the King's River, which was not as large as Table Rock Lake, I thought to myself, I would like to take a canoe trip down this river.

When we drove through Holiday Island on Route 23 on the way to north Main Street, I said to Anna Marie, "This small village would be an ideal place to live. It is near Table Rock Lake and Eureka Springs."

Five miles later I drove into Eureka Springs. Across from the railroad station, I took the first turn to the right on Grand Avenue. Then a first left on Dairy Hollow to Spring Street. We arrived around noon at the Crescent Hotel.

"Here we are," I said to Anna Marie

I parked my car in the hotel's parking lot. The lot was nearly full, but I found a place at the back.

"I am so excited!" said Anna Marie. "We're finally here."

"Yes, we are," I said as I opened the car door. I walked to the trunk and opened it to take out our suitcases. I took two suitcases, one blue and one red, out of the trunk. Anna Marie lifted the handle of her red suitcase and began walking towards the hotel. I did the same with my suitcase. As we approached the hotel, we paused.

"It's huge," said Anna Marie.

"I agree. I see five stories," I said, "Let's check in."

As we approached the massive entrance, a doorman opened the door.

"Welcome to the Crescent Hotel," said the young man.

"Thank you," I said.

"The registration table is on your left as you enter the building."

As we entered the hotel, we paused and looked around the lobby. My eyes were drawn straight ahead to the large door that opened to the south porch and veranda overlooking Eureka Springs. The sun was streaming through the glass. As I turned to my right, I saw a huge stone fireplace with a warm fire burning and Victorian furniture facing the fireplace.

"Impressive!" I said to Anna Marie. Then I looked to my left and saw the wooden registration office. We walked to the counter and gave our names.

After registering, we walked up the stairs to the fourth floor to room 422. The room was decorated with Victorian furniture, a mirror, and curtains. Thankfully, the small bathroom had modern plumbing. We shared a room that had two twin beds. We unpacked our suitcases and hung our clothes on hangers in the closet.

"Ghost sightings were seen on this floor," said Anna Marie, "I hope I see a ghost."

I thought to myself that I didn't want to see a ghost. I was feeling nervous and anxious.

"I am so excited!" said Anna Marie. "We are really here, in a haunted hotel! My dream has come true."

After unpacking we walked down the stairs to register for the ESP workshop. A woman sat at a desk in the lobby with an ESP registration sign. We were given a schedule that listed the times and events of the workshop. She pointed to the schedule and said, "The workshop will begin at 3:00 this afternoon in the Conservatory." She also gave us a pamphlet which gave a short history of the hotel.

"I'm hungry," I said to Anna Marie, "Let's go eat at the restaurant, Dr. Baker's Bistro and Sky Bar, on the top floor of the hotel."

"Good idea! We can read the information about the workshop while we're eating," I replied. Once again we walked up the stairs, since the Bistro was on the highest floor.

"I wish the elevator was repaired," Anna Marie said, "I'm not used to walking up stairs." They found the restaurant crowded, with no tables available.

"I wonder if all these people are attending the ESP workshop," I said to Anna Marie.

"I wonder, too," she said. "There must be a lot of interest in ghost stories."

After a wait of five minutes, we found an empty table and sat down. A waitress appeared and gave us menus and asked what we wanted to drink.

"I want a cup of coffee, no cream," I replied.

"I'll have a diet coke," said Anna Marie. We looked over the menu wondering what to select. The waitress arrived with our drinks and asked what we had selected.

"I'll have a hamburger with fries," said Anna Marie.

"I would like a Reuben sandwich with apple sauce." While waiting for the food to arrive, I looked at the pamphlet describing the hotel.

"This should interest you, Anna Marie; this pamphlet says that 'The Crescent Hotel has been called America's Most Haunted Hotel, and is said to be haunted by at least eight spirits.' Did you know eight ghosts have been seen?"

"Yes," said Anna Marie, "That is one of the reasons for coming to this hotel and attending this workshop. As I was looking at the ESP workshop materials, I noticed that there would be a tour of the parts of the hotel where the ghosts have been seen. We will even go to the basement to see the morgue."

Our meals arrived, and both of us ate quickly. The food was delicious and filling.

"I may need to take a nap," I said to Ana Marie. "Let's go to our room and rest until it is time to attend the workshop."

"Good idea," said Anna Marie. We left the restaurant and walked to our rooms.

I took off my shoes, pulled the bedspread back from the bed, and lay down. As I was resting, I looked around the room. On the wall there were a couple of old portraits of a man and a woman. It seemed that the eyes of the man were looking at me. I laughed and thought my imagination was getting the best of me.

Anna Marie heard me laugh and asked, "Why are you laughing?"

I turned my head towards her and said, "For a minute, I thought the man's eyes were looking at me. Isn't that absurd?" I laughed again.

Anna Marie looked at the portrait and said, "I thought he was looking at me. I was feeling anxious just looking at him."

We both laughed.

Chapter Six

After a relaxing rest, Anna Marie and I walked downstairs at 2:45 p.m. to the lobby and the room where the meeting would be held. The room had many windows with the sunlight streaming in. I wondered if originally this room might have been a conservatory for plants or for music. As I looked around, I noticed that there were about twenty people in attendance; the average age seemed to be around fifty. There were several older couples and a few couples younger than me. One couple sitting behind me seemed to be "attached at the hip" as the saying goes. They seemed more interested in each other than the program. The man—about thirty-five years old—had his right arm around her shoulders and held her hand with his left hand. They were looking at each other, whispering and giggling. Both of them were wearing jeans and sweaters.

At 3:00 a man in his sixties stood up at a podium and

introduced himself. He was wearing dark trousers and a dark jacket over a white shirt with an open collar. His hair was turning gray, and his eyes were dark brown.

He smiled and said, "Welcome to the Crescent Hotel and the ESP workshop. My name is Fred Von Briesen. I am the coordinator for the ESP workshops. Also, I lead ghost tours every evening and on weekends. We will have two opportunities to go on a ghost tour. The first one will be at this hotel. The second one will be at the Basin Park Hotel, a hotel that is also owned by the owner of the Crescent Hotel. Ghosts have been reported to have been seen at both places. I will lead you on these two ghost tours; hopefully, you will see a ghost."

Fred looked around the room to see if the workshop participants were listening. They seemed interested, so he continued his presentation.

"In 2005, Jason Hawes and Grant Wilson, presenters of the television show *Ghost Hunters,* visited the Crescent Hotel and recorded a full-body apparition on their thermal imaging camera; the form seemed to be that of a man wearing a hat and nodding his head. Do we need any more proof than their photos to state that there are ghosts in the Crescent Hotel? Now, open your program brochure and let's go over the schedule. This afternoon the program will end at 5:00. Dinner will be served in the Crystal Ballroom at 6:00. The workshop will continue at 7:00 p.m. Notice in the program that there are two speakers for this workshop. Let me introduce them at this time. They are Jerry Weisland and Donna Jewett. Jerry and Donna have been married for twenty years and live in Denver, Colorado. Donna is a psychic consultant, lecturer on paranormal topics, hypnotherapist and past life therapist, and investigator of psychic ghosts. Jerry is a ghost investigator and uses equipment similar to the Ghost Hunters on television."

Donna was wearing a large flowing dark blue robe over dark trousers. She wore several rings on her fingers which had large stones of various colors: purple amethyst, clear diamond, and dark blue lapis. Around her neck she wore a large crystal pendant on a gold chain.

Donna stood up and said, "Thank you for the introduction. I am happy to be here to share my experiences with you and go on the ghost tours of the Crescent and Basin Hotel. I have been a psychic for the past thirty years. I have a master's degree in psychology and received training to be a hypnotherapist. While practicing and teaching psychology at a local community college in Denver, I was invited to attend an ESP conference in Fort Collins. At that conference, I attended a workshop session, 'Discover Your Psychic Abilities,' led by a noted psychic from California. From doing various exercises to learn psychic skills, I discovered that I was a natural psychic. The instructor suggested that I study with her. I was surprised yet excited. I took a leave of absence from my teaching position and spent the second semester and summer in California learning to develop my skills. My teacher was very skillful and intuitive. I returned to my teaching position for the fall semester. I also began using my psychic skills in my private practice. For the next five years my psychic private practice grew and became very successful. I resigned my teaching position so that I could work full-time as a psychic consultant. While teaching psychology at the community college, I met my husband, Jerry."

Turning to Jerry, she said, "I turn the podium over to you."

Donna sat down and Jerry stood up and walked to the podium. Jerry was wearing blue jeans and a gray wool jacket over a light blue shirt with an open collar.

"Thank you, Donna. How fortunate I am to be married to Donna. I found a companion to share my interests. Donna can sense ghosts in a room; I use my equipment. The equipment that I use as a ghost investigator include: digital thermometers, EMF meters, thermographic and night vision cameras, handheld and static digital video cameras, and digital audio recorders. These photos and recordings are linked to my laptop computer. The operating system on my laptop is updated at least every two years. The ghost hunters on the television show introduced a couple of new pieces during their fifth season. One was a custom-made geophone, which detects vibrations and flashes a series of LEDs that measure the intensity of the vibration. The second was a new EMF detector that makes a buzzing sound when in the presence of an electromagnetic field; the stronger the field, the louder it buzzes. In one episode, the geophones were recorded on video flashing to the vibrations of what sounded like footsteps across a floor, even though no one was apparently in the room.

"When Donna and I are asked to investigate ghosts or paranormal activity, we first check the internet to see what historical information about the town or building we can find. Second, we set up an appointment with the person who has asked us to investigate. On arrival in the nearest city or town, we check into a hotel to spend several days. Then, we visit and survey the property with the owner. The owner's experiences with the reported sightings are recorded. Next, we set up the electronic equipment in the rooms where the sightings of ghosts have been reported. While I watch the equipment, Donna walks around the room and tunes into any ghosts in the room. We spend two days recording any ghostly activity. Then we go to our hotel, and spend several days analyzing the data. After reviewing the data, we share the findings with the owner.

"We do not always find ghosts. Sometimes the explanation is a natural cause such as mice moving in a room or lights flashing from a passing car. If there is some evidence of a ghost, Donna shares with the owner what he or she can do to get rid of the apparition. Or sometimes she will do a cleansing of the room and ask the ghost to leave. However, some hotels advertise, like the Crescent Hotel, that they have ghosts. Many people are drawn to a hotel where they may experience any paranormal activity. Are there any questions?"

Many hands were raised by the participants. For the next hour questions were raised and then answered by Jerry and Donna. At 5:00 p.m. Fred stood up and announced the end of the afternoon session. "Dinner will be at 6:00, and we will continue our workshop at 7:00 p.m."

Following the workshop, Anna Marie and I walked up the stairs to our room to rest. I said to her, "What do you think of the program so far? Jerry is really handsome and charming. I would like to get acquainted with him."

She replied, "I am so pleased that Donna and Jerry are

the presenters and investigators of ghosts. I didn't expect to have experts with us this weekend."

"I agree. Donna and Jerry are impressive! I may actually see a ghost."

When we walked into the Crystal Dining Room, I looked up and saw the beautiful crystal chandeliers. I was in awe. The hostess escorted us to a corner of the room to the two tables where the ESP workshop group was assigned. Anna Marie and I sat next to each other. On my left, an older woman sat down.

"My name is Judy Mowrey." She said. "I'm a writer from Little Rock. I arrived with my partner, Julie Sands, who is sitting to my left."

I introduced myself, followed by Anna Marie. A couple in their sixties sat across from us. He introduced himself by saying, "Hello, my name is Alfred Schneider" He turned to his right and said, "This is my wife, Heide Schneider. We live in Kansas City. We enjoy visiting haunted hotels. We hope to see a ghost this weekend."

"Don't we all," chimed in Judy Mowry.

Next to the Schneiders sat a young woman who looked about thirty years old. She had long blonde hair and a petite figure.

She introduced herself. "Hi, I'm Sandy Parks. I like reading ghost stories. I live in St. Louis. Next to me is

Arnold Marshall."

Arnold looked to be around thirty to forty years old, average height with bleached hair and a dark mustache. He was wearing an expensive looking jacket with an open collar, and wearing a gold chain with a cross around his neck.

Arnold said, "We met at a local bar several months ago and have become very good friends. We discovered that we enjoy reading murder mysteries and ghost stories. But I'm not so sure I want to meet a ghost."

Seated next to Arnold was June. She was in her late twenties, tall, and dressed in black.

"Hi, my name is June. I am an aspiring writer from Eureka Springs. I've been taking writing classes at the Eureka Springs Writers' Colony. I work at one of the jewelry shops in town during the day. During the evening I write mysteries and ghost stories."

The next person to speak was a tall, thin, dark- skinned woman. She was wearing a red, long sleeved wool dress and black knee boots. Around her neck she wore a gold chain necklace.

In a deep low voice she said, "Hello everyone, I am pleased to meet you. My name is Juliet. I am a cocktail waitress at a hotel in Jonesboro. I am here with my friend sitting next to me."

She pointed to a tall man in his thirties, wearing dark rimmed glasses, a white shirt, and jeans. He had strawberry blonde hair and blue eyes.

"My name is John. I am a short story writer from Jonesboro."

Just then a waiter came to our table and handed each of us a menu.

"What would you like to drink?" he asked.

I replied, "I would like a glass of chardonnay."

Anna Marie said, "Make that two."

The other guests said they would like wine as well. Alfred ordered a bottle of Merlot, and Judy and Julie ordered a white, house wine. The special of the day was prime rib with garlic mashed potatoes. Since I don't like garlic, which is another story, I ordered a grilled tuna. After everyone ordered their meal and drank a glass of wine, the conversation at the table centered around ghost stories.

After dinner we walked to the meeting room. Anna Marie and I sat next to Judy and Julie.

The evening program consisted of watching a couple of television shows of ghost hunting. One of the shows was the one where the ghost investigators came to the Crescent Hotel. After the shows, there were many questions raised. For the next hour Jerry and Donna answered the questions. The program concluded at 9:00 p.m. Anna

Marie and I stood up with the rest of the group.

Anna Marie said, "It's too early to go to our rooms. What shall we do?"

I agreed.

Judy, who sat next to me, said, "Let's go upstairs to the bar, Dr. Baker's Bistro, and have a drink?"

"Good idea," I said.

Anna Marie and I followed Judy and Julie up the stairs to the Bistro. The room was crowded, but we found one remaining table in the back of the room. All of us ordered beer and nachos. Around 10:00 we left the Bistro and walked to our rooms. Ann Marie and I spent the next hour talking about the people and the program. Then Anna Marie immediately went to sleep.

I had a difficult time falling asleep. I kept hearing noises and imagined seeing things. Are there ghosts in the room? I asked myself. Speaking out loud, I said, "Is there anyone in the room?" I waited for an answer. Nothing happened. I listened and looked around. Anna Marie was sound asleep and did not hear me speaking. I turned on the light and started reading a book that I had brought with me. The book was written by one of my favorite murder mystery authors. I tried reading, but still kept hearing noises. After looking all around the room, I realized that there were tree limbs brushing against the window, and I finally relaxed. I put my book down, turned off the light, and in a few minutes I was fast asleep.

Chapter Seven

After a difficult night's sleep, dealing with ghosts and demons in my dreams, I finally awoke when the alarm went off. I dressed quickly, put on my jeans, a blue sweater, and a jean jacket. Anna Marie was already dressed. She was also wearing jeans, a green sweater and a gray jacket. She was sitting at the desk in the room reading.

"Good morning, Sue. About time you awoke. The time is 8:00 a.m. Remember, the workshop starts at 9:00 a.m."

"Thanks, Anna Marie, I had a difficult night—too many dreams."

"Let's go eat."

"Good idea! I'm hungry." We walked down the stairs to the dining room and sat at a table with some of the other workshop members.

"Good morning," I said. "Did you all sleep well?"

The responses were varied from "no" to "yes."

A breakfast buffet was set up. Anna Marie and I walked to the buffet table and filled our plates. We were hungry.

At 9:00 a.m. we walked into the meeting room. Not every workshop participant was in attendance. Maybe they had slept in.

Fred was standing in front of the room. "Good morning. I hope all of you slept well. Did anyone see a ghost?" No one raised their hand. "This morning, Donna and Jerry will speak on *Orbs*."

"Good morning," said Donna as she walked to the front of the room. I want to give you a definition of *Orbs*."

Besides investigating ghosts and spirits, we also investigate spirit orbs. Some people say that a spirit orb is a snapshot of the past. Others say that an orb is outside this reality, a psychic phenomenon that people witness. I believe that when the energy lines are balanced and the energy centers increase, paranormal activity such as orbs occur. Orbs occur where there is a high energy vibration. Jerry will pass around a scrapbook of photos that hotel residents have taken of orbs and ghosts. Have any of you seen any orbs?" Several hands rose.

Suddenly the door to the meeting room opened and the Sheriff and a Deputy walked into the room.

"Sorry for the interruption," said the Sheriff, "but a murder has occurred. One of the members of this workshop was murdered last night. His name is John. Do any of you know him?"

Fred Von Briesen spoke up, "Sheriff, I'm Fred Von Briesen, the program director for the hotel. I have a little information about John. He registered for the workshop giving his home address and telephone number. That's all the information that we have. He had a friend, Juliet, with him, but she's not here this morning."

"Thanks," said the Sheriff. "I want to interview each one of you. As of now, the workshop has been suspended. I know you're disappointed, but finding the murderer is a priority. No one will be allowed to leave this hotel until further notice. I will begin interviewing each one of you in this room. All of you go to the lounge and wait until you're called.

As Anna Marie and I waited our turn to be interviewed, we sat by the fireplace and talked about the murder.

"What do we know about John? What connection does he have with any members of this group besides Juliet?"

Ann Marie replied, "I have no idea. What I do know is that a ghost would not be carrying a gun, so that rules them out."

I laughed and said, "I don't think the Sheriff ever considered a ghost as the murderer."

When the Sheriff called my name, I walked into the

meeting room. The sheriff pointed to an empty chair and suggested that I sit there for the interview.

"Did you know John?" asked the sheriff.

"Only from this workshop," I replied. "He and Juliet were a couple. They didn't talk in the workshop. They sat in the last row. During our break time and lunch time I saw John talking to a couple, Sandy and Arnold.

"Do you know what they were talking about?"

"Not really. However, it seemed that Sandy and John did most of the talking. Arnold was quiet."

"Thank you, Sue. You've been most helpful."

When I left the room, I heard the Sheriff call for Anna Marie to be interviewed.

After her interview I said to her, "What did you say to the Sheriff?"

"I gave him very little information. The only information I gave was my personal view of John. I said that he was good looking and seemed to be a scholarly person. Maybe it was because he wore glasses."

Together we walked up the stairs to our room. On our floor, we noticed that the Deputy and two other policemen were standing in the room that must have been John's. As we walked by we heard the Deputy say to one of the policemen, "Don't forget to call the Memphis Police Department."

I was startled by the comment—the Memphis Police Department? Why would they want to be in contact with the Memphis Police Department? Several hours later I learned the reason.

While Anna Marie and I were sitting by the fireplace in the lounge area of the hotel, several policemen opened the door to the hotel and walked to the registration area. I noticed that they were from the Memphis, Tennessee Police Department.

"Where's the Carroll County Sheriff?" asked one of the policemen to a person in the registration area.

"He's in the conservatory room to your right," the employee replied.

During the dinner hour the workshop participants sat together in the dining room. Several bottles of wine were ordered. Most people sat quietly eating their meal and drinking a lot of wine. Judy told a joke and the group politely laughed, however, no one followed with another joke or story.

Anna Marie and I wondered what we could do for the rest of the evening. We decided to go to our room and spend the evening reading or watching television. I found a British mystery on public television. I spent the next hour watching the show. I usually gain some new ideas for my novels from watching British murder mysteries and looked forward to the next hour of the program. After the movie I still wasn't sleepy. I picked up my mystery novel from the bedside table and began reading.

Around midnight, I finally fell asleep. Dreams of murder suspects ran through my mind throughout the night.

Chapter Eight

The night was uneventful. I slept well in spite of dreams of murder suspects. As I looked out the window I observed a light snow falling.

"I wonder what the weather forecast will be," I said to Anna Marie.

"Let's turn on the television set and watch the weather report," she replied.

"Good idea," I said and turned on the weather report. The forecast predicted a forty percent chance of light snow for the Northwest section of Arkansas.

"That's good news," I said. "Let's go downstairs for breakfast. I need a cup of coffee."

We walked down the stairs to the dining room to join the workshop group. I noticed that Sandy and Arnold were absent.

"Where are Sandy and Arnold?" I asked the group.

"Haven't you heard?" replied Alfred, "Early this morning Sandy was found dead, lying in the snow. The police think that she died from falling off the balcony."

"How awful!" I responded. "When did it happen?"

June said, "I heard that it happened late last night. My guess is that she had been drinking and accidently fell. What a coincidence, two murders during an ESP workshop!"

"I don't believe in coincidences," I said. "There's a lot going on that we are unaware of. My guess is that Sandy was murdered."

"How can you say that," replied Alfred, "You have no evidence that points to her being murdered."

"No, I don't, but I think there's a connection between the two murders," I said.

"I couldn't sleep last night," said June, "I went to the bar for a drink. In a dark corner of the room, I saw Sandy and our instructor, Jerry Wallace, having drinks. Maybe Jerry had something to do with Sandy's death."

"Have you given this information to the Sheriff? This information is vital for the police to solve the murder," I said.

"Yes, I'll give the information to the Sheriff," said June, "I realize that any clue is important."

"Where is Arnold?" I asked.

"The Sheriff is interviewing him at this moment in the conservatory. Since Arnold and June are close friends, he may know what happened."

After breakfast we were told to wait in the lounge until the Sheriff called us in for an interview. This interview with the Sheriff will be about the same as yesterday since I have no additional information to give to him. While we were waiting for our interviews, Arnold walked out of the conservatory holding a handkerchief to his eyes.

"How are you doing?" I asked him. "It's so sad that Sandy fell, a tragic death. Is there anything we can do to help you?"

"Thanks, I appreciate your concern. Sandy and I were very close. I miss her. There's nothing anyone can do until the Sheriff has completed his interviews."

Ten minutes later, I was called in for my interview. The Sheriff asked, "Do you have any information that can help us identify the murderer of Jason or of Sandy?"

"No, I don't. So, you believe Sandy was murdered as well?"

"Yes, we found marks around her neck. Someone strangled her and pushed her over the edge of the balcony."

"That is so sad and scary. Are we murder suspects, or will one of us be the next victim?" I asked.

"Yes, all of you are murder suspects, and I can't promise

you that there will be no more murders."

"Is there anything else you want from me?" I asked.

"No, but don't leave the hotel."

I walked out of the room and asked Anna Marie to join me for some coffee. Coffee was provided for the guests on the south side of the lobby. As we were talking, Fred Von Hiesen walked into the lobby and joined us. He poured a cup of coffee and sat across from us.

"I'm sorry that the workshop had to be canceled because of these terrible murders," Fred said. "This has never happened before. I don't know what to do."

"Have you ever been to a séance?" I asked.

"No, I have not," answered Fred. "I'm not sure if we can communicate with ghosts or the deceased."

"I have an idea. What if we held a séance and the two murder victims appeared? Do you suppose that would lead the murderer in our workshop to reveal him or herself?"

"Hmm, I am beginning to see what you're suggesting. Donna has experience in contacting spirits or ghosts. I'll talk to her about conducting a séance," said Fred. "Maybe we can plan to have one this evening. I'll let you know."

Fred stood up and walked over to Donna and Jerry. They had not been interviewed by the Sheriff as yet.

"Donna, I would like to talk to you. Will you come with me to my office?"

"Yes," said Donna. She stood up and followed Fred to his office.

I looked at Anna Marie and said, "I wish I was a mouse, so that I could follow them into Fred' office and hear their conversations."

"I hope they're planning a séance to expose the murderer," I said.

"If they're planning a séance, do you think the murderer will be exposed?" asked Anna Marie.

"I hope so. Otherwise, we may have to stay at this hotel until the Sheriff finds the killer."

After thirty minutes, Donna left Fred's office. She walked into the Conservatory and talked to the Sheriff. He excused himself from the person he was interviewing and walked out of the room to Fred's office. Once again, I wished I was a mouse so that I could hear what was being said in Fred's office.

Noontime approached and I was beginning to realize that I was hungry. "Let's have lunch," I said to Anna Marie.

"Good idea! I'm hungry too," Anna Marie said.

At the lunch table Fred made an announcement. "At 7:00 p.m. tonight, we'll continue our workshop by having a séance. Since Donna has experience contacting spirits, she has offered to conduct the séance. We will meet in the conservatory."

After Fred left the table, participants began talking to one another.

Judy Mowrey said, "I don't think it's appropriate to continue the workshop. Two people have been murdered."

"I think it is a good idea to have a séance," said Alfred. "After all, I registered for this workshop hoping that I would see a ghost or sense a spirit."

"I'm not interested in attending the séance," said Arnold. "Maybe some evil spirits will show up. I read my horoscope today, and it warned me to beware of group gatherings."

"Don't worry, there are no evil spirits," said June, "There are only good spirits."

"I wish I could believe that, but I'm sorry; I don't. I'm uncomfortable with the possibility of evil spirits," said Arnold as he kissed the cross that hung around his neck.

The other workshop members discussed the pros and cons of having a séance.

Finally, I said, "Look, I'm tired; I'm going to my room to rest for a couple hours. The séance is planned, and all of us have to attend. I think the Sheriff will be there to make sure that we all attend." I stood up and walked out of the dining room followed by Anna Marie.

"Wait for me, I'll join you," she said.

We walked up the stairs to our room and tried to take a

nap, but instead of sleeping, I read my mystery novel.

After Judy and Fred had a talk in Fred's office, Judy looked for Jerry. She found him sitting at the bar drinking a beer and talking to some of the workshop participants.

"Jerry, I want to talk to you. Let's go to our room for some privacy."

"I'll be up in a minute. I want to finish my beer."

"Okay, I'll be in our room."

Judy walked upstairs to their room. She walked to the closet and took out a black gown to wear for the séance. "I want to look the part of a medium. This black gown will work," she said to herself. She held the gown in front of her as she looked into the mirror. "Not bad." Five minutes later, Jerry walked into the room.

"Is there a problem?" asked Jerry.

"No, should there be?" replied Donna.

"When you asked me to come to the room, you had a serious look on your face? Are you concerned that I had a beer with the workshop participants?"

"No, but I had wondered why you were sitting so close to June. The reason I wanted to talk to you concerns your equipment to measure spirits and ghosts. I want you to set up your equipment for the séance tonight."

"Sure, I can do that. I was wondering when I would have the opportunity. Shall I set up all of the equipment or just the recording device?"

"Set up all the equipment," said Donna.

"I'll need at least an hour to set it all up," said Jerry, "We'll have to eat an early dinner."

"That sounds good; let's eat a salad at 5:30 in the Bistro. That should give us time to be ready for the séance."

After dinner Jerry and Donna brought all the equipment down the stairs to the conservatory. Donna helped Jerry set up the equipment. At 6:15 Donna left to go to her room to dress and put on make-up. If there was time, she would try to spend some moments in meditation.

Chapter Nine

At 6:45 Donna walked into the conservatory dressed in black. A large clear crystal hung around her neck on a gold chain. Jerry followed her dressed in his usual clothes, dark jeans, a white shirt, and a jacket.

Donna said to Jerry, "Please arrange twenty chairs in a circle. You and I will sit at opposite ends. We will follow a similar procedure in setting up a séance. We will set up a small table in the center with a lighted candle. All of the lights in the room will be turned out. At 7:00 all the participants will be asked to sit in the circle. Ask the Sheriff and Deputy as well as Fred to sit outside the circle."

As the group participants walked into the room, Jerry asked them to sit down in a chair in the circle, on either side of Donna. No one sat in Jerry's chair since he had hung his jacket on the back.

As everyone sat down Donna said, "Please hold the

hands of the person to the left and right of you. I will call upon the spirits, and then go into a trance. If contact is made with me, the spirits may speak through me. Are there any questions before we get started?"

Everyone looked at each other wondering if anyone would have the courage to ask a question. No one spoke.

"If there are no questions, I shall proceed with the séance," said Donna. She lit the candle with a match, and asked Jerry to turn out the lights.

Before Donna began invoking any spirits, I noticed that my hands and the hands on either side of me were moist. I was nervous and tense. My guess was that everyone one else holding hands felt the same.

"Oh Mother Goddess, we ask for your guidance and protection tonight. Protect us from those spirits whose intentions are less than desirable. Help us tune in to those spirits who have recently passed over. Give them comfort and guidance to communicate with us. *CALL UPON THOSE SPIRITS TO SPEAK*. Is anyone there? Please show yourself."

Suddenly the candle began to flicker, and it went out. The room was very dark.

One of Jerry's detection machines began to make a loud noise. Some people jumped; others shivered.

Donna spoke, "I shall put myself in a trance so you can

speak through me."

She took several breaths and became quiet. A few minutes later, she spoke in a low masculine voice, "One of you present tonight killed me. I shall seek revenge. You can't escape me."

"Get away from me—don't hurt me," yelled a man's voice. A man jumped up from his seat and ran towards the door. The lights were turned on by the Sheriff. The Deputy had Arnold's hands cuffed.

"Why did you kill John?" asked the Sheriff.

"He recognized me from a drug bust in Memphis. I shot him in Memphis, but apparently he recovered and followed me here. Saturday evening after the workshop, he stopped me and said that I looked familiar; but sooner or later I knew he would recognize me. I suggested that we meet later for a beer, after I said goodnight to Sandy. We met at the bar, and I pointed a gun at him that was hidden under my jacket. I told him to walk down to the basement. As I was ready to shove him inside a small room, he grabbed me and scratched my hands. I took out my gun and shot him in the forehead. He died immediately. Quickly I ran up the stairs to my room. No one saw me. The next evening I saw Sandy having a drink with Jerry. I thought that they were having an affair. I asked her to come to my room to talk. I confronted her about having an affair, and she laughed."

She said. "I should ask you the same question and where did you go after you left me last night?"

"She kept teasing me and laughing. I didn't think the situation was funny, so I hit her. She fell to the floor. She said that she would complain to the police about me hitting her. I kept hitting her and then put my hands around her neck until she became quiet. Her face was bloody, and she was no longer breathing. I didn't know what to do. Finally, around 1:00 in the morning I opened the window in my room and threw her body out of the window. The next day when her body was found, the police thought she had fallen from the balcony. Later, they realized that she had been murdered."

The Sheriff left the room, followed by the Deputy and Arnold with his hands cuffed. As they left Juliet walked through the door, wearing a police badge, jeans, and a black leather jacket.

"Let me explain what has happened. First of all, my name is Jackie. John, whose birth name is Jason, and I worked together as undercover detectives to expose a drug ring in Memphis. We finally got a tip that Arnold, or his name in Memphis—Carlos, was the ringleader. As we were ready to arrest Carlos, he escaped by shooting Jason in the shoulder. After months of searching, we received a lead that Carlos was in St. Louis. Jason drove to St. Louis, and learned that Carlos was planning to attend the ESP workshop at the Crescent. Jason and I disguised ourselves, and joined the participants at the workshop. We were planning to arrest Carlos as soon as we recognized him. Carlos was wearing a good disguise, but the gold chain and cross gave him away. We knew Carlos always carried a gun, so we had to find a way to arrest him without him shooting anyone. However, our plan failed. Carlos had discovered who Jason was and murdered him. The Sheriff contacted me and told me about the séance. I was waiting outside the Conservatory to arrest Carlos."

Fred appeared in the room from behind a curtain.

I said, "What was the plan?"

"I'll explain. Earlier today Donna and I talked with the Sheriff about exposing the murderer. I suggested that Donna pretend to have a séance. I would use a fan to blow out the candle. Donna would ask Jerry to turn on one of his machines to make a noise as if a ghost or spirit had arrived. It worked, thanks to Donna and Jerry."

"What a great idea, Fred," said Donna, "I enjoyed playing the role of a medium leading a séance."

"You mean that you have never led a séance before, Donna?" Fred exclaimed.

"That's right. I have personally contacted spirits, but

never called upon a spirit or ghost during a séance," Donna replied.

"Did we have a real séance or not?" I asked.

"I'll check my recording devices to see if any ghost or spirit appeared in the room," said Jerry. He walked over to his equipment and checked the infrared camera first. To his shock there was an outline of a heat signature standing in the center of the circle.

"Oh, my gosh," said Jerry, "there was something here in the room with us!"

"Finally, a ghost appeared!" said Alfred. "Although I didn't see anything, there is proof that spirits or ghosts exist."

Epilogue

Monday morning all of us left the Crescent Hotel to go to our respective homes. On the drive back to Springfield, Anna Marie and I discussed the weekend, trying to analyze any clues that we might have noticed, or anything that pointed to the murderer.

"I was taken completely by surprise. I had no idea that Arnold had a previous history with the murder victim," I said. I felt sorry for Donna, who didn't know she was in a relationship with a criminal.

"One positive thing did come from the workshop. We finally had a ghost appear," said Anna Marie, "although I didn't see it."

"I'm glad that I didn't see it," I said. "If I had, I would have probably screamed."

"Our experiences this weekend may turn into a good murder and ghost mystery," said Anna Marie.

"Well, I'm not ready to write the story," I said. "You can write it.

CHARACTERS IN ORDER OF APPEARANCE

Myrtle, the maid who found the body

Rachel Beth, friend of Myrtle

Jim, front desk worker

Manager of the hotel

Sheriff

Deputy

Coroner

Jason Pierson, "Hal" – detective and murder victim

Jackie Larsen, undercover policewoman, friend of

Jason

Nate, Drug Dealer

Carlos, Drug Leader

Detective Haley, St. Louis Police Department

Bartender in St. Louis

Fred Von Briesen, Program Director of ESP Workshop

Ginger Van Briesen, Wife of Fred Van Briesen

Donna Jewett, Workshop Presenter

Jerry Weisfield, Husband of Donna and Presenter

Doorman

Workshop Participants:

Anna Marie, housewife and friend from Springfield, MO

Sue Henry, author, first person voice, Springfield, MO

Judy Mowrey, novelist, Little Rock

Julie Sands, partner to Judy, Little Rock

Alfred and Heide Schneider, Kansas City, MO.

Arnold Marshall, St. Louis

Sandy Parks, St. Louis, friend of Arnold

June Bowen, Eureka Springs

Juliet, Cocktail Waitress, Jonesburg

John, writer, Jonesburg

Five other participants, not named

MURDER
AT THE OZARK UFO
CONFERENCE

Dedication

This book is dedicated to all the people I have met who have told me their stories of being abducted by an UFO.

I want to thank Dan Krotz, a fellow writer, who suggested the idea to write a murder mystery story with the UFO conference as the setting.

Introduction

UFOs have always been an interest. I was a loyal fan of the *X-Files*. I wanted to believe that there were aliens visiting earth. *The truth is out there*. Also, while visiting England a few years ago I saw a Crop Circle in a field near Avery. Are these phenomenon created by UFOs? Our tour guide believed they were.

While attending a conference in Virginia twenty years ago, I met a man who told me his story of seeing an UFO. One night as he and his army buddy were walking home from a club, they saw a bright light following them. Quickly they ducked into a ditch. They believed that they saw an UFO. Because of the common belief that UFOs were untrue, they did not disclose their sighting until years later. They were afraid that people would think they were drunk.

During the 70s and 80s UFOs were sighted around the world. Articles, organizations, and conferences were held sharing the information.

A couple years ago I attended the Ozark UFO Conference in Eureka Springs. From listening to speakers and watching videos, the experiences made me a believer. Also, I met Delores Cannon, the Director of the conference for that year. Delores spent 45 years as a hypnotherapist and past life regressionist. She spoke about her experiences with clients that regressed to past lives on other planets or planes of existence. At the conference I bought some of her books and delved into them.

This story is a fictional account of my experiences attending an Ozark UFO Conference.

Chapter One

"I was abducted by aliens," said Tom, one of the members of the Mystery Writers' Club that was meeting in Springfield, Missouri. "Initially, I thought I was dreaming. This experience could not be real. Then I had other abduction experiences; I began to think that I was going crazy. Finally, I sought out a hypnotherapist who worked with other abductees. Though hypnotherapy I was able to understand that many of my abductions occurred in my unconscious as out-of-body experiences. There was no alien ship that abducted me."

As he was talking about his abductions, questions kept coming into my mind. Are UFOs real? Are aliens visiting our planet? Are abductions real or a dream experience? I remember reading a book about aliens visiting our planet several thousand years ago. It was written by a Swiss author, Erich von Daniken. Also, I have watched a History Channel program about aliens visiting the earth.

"While living in Eureka Springs, Arkansas, I had numerous experiences of being abducted," continued Tom. "I met other people who also talked about their abductions. Many people asked me to write about my experiences. Finally, I relented and sent a manuscript to a publisher. The book was published and is for sale on Amazon."

"How can I find more information about UFOs?" I asked.

Tom answered, "Sue, to find out more information about UFOs, you can search the internet, read books, or attend the annual Ozark UFO Conference in Eureka Springs, Arkansas held the second weekend of April."

"Thanks, Tom."

After the meeting, I talked to my friend, Anna Marie, about the possibilities of attending the UFO Conference in Eureka Springs. Anna Marie and I have been close friends for a long time. We met at a nursery school where our oldest children were enrolled. She had a son and a daughter around the same ages as my two sons. We began to socialize by bringing our families together. Now that our children are grown and out-of-the-house, Anna Marie and I have joined a Writers' Group. We are learning to write stories and one day write the great American novel.

Primarily, I like to write about murder mysteries; Anna Marie also likes to write murder mysteries and ghost stories. Every time we drive past an old Victorian house, she will say, "I wonder if there are any ghosts living in that house."

A year ago we had the opportunity to attend an ESP workshop in Eureka Springs and stay in a one hundred year old haunted hotel. We didn't see any ghosts but we were told that there was one in the workshop room. That weekend was filled with ghost stories and murder mysteries.

Anna Marie was as excited about attending the UFO Conference as I was. We needed some inspiration to write our next story. The UFO Conference may be the place to provide us with some ideas. We decided to check for more information on-line and then share the information.

Eureka Springs is one of my favorite destinations. It has been designated a historical village with many Victorian homes and hotels. The town was based on the numerous springs where people were healed. As word of Eureka's miraculous, healing waters began to spread during the 1800s, thousands of visitors flocked to the original encampment of tents and hastily built shanties. During the 1900s, the springs became polluted and people no longer came to Eureka Springs. Then new sewer systems were installed and the springs, once again, drew tourists to the town. Now, the town has around 2,500 citizens. The greater Eureka Springs area has around 6,000 people. Eureka Springs has many walking trails from one spring to another. The Parks and Recreation Commission maintain gardens around the springs. Each time I visit the town I like to walk to the springs and see what flowers are blooming in the gardens.

I quickly drove home and turned on my computer. I typed in Ozark UFO Conference. All sorts of information popped up. I looked at the schedule and the speakers. A statement in the information enticed me: *Take the journey with us and explore the possibilities of the universe and beyond.* I was ready to sign up and explore the possibilities of the universe and beyond.

The conference was a three day event held in April at the Inn of the Ozarks in Eureka Springs. The conference was a month away, still time to register. Immediately, I called Anna Marie.

"Anna Marie, I'm so excited; I plan to attend the conference!"

"Me too! I read over the schedule and found the topics intriguing," said Anna Marie.

"Since it's only a month away, I'll call the conference office and register both of us online. I'll pay the registration fees and you can pay me back later. While I'm doing that, why don't you call the conference hotel, the Best Western Inn of the Ozarks, and see if you can get a room?"

"Good planning, Sue, I'll do that immediately. I'll talk to you later."

Before registering for the conference I poured a cup of coffee to help me calm down. I was so excited! As I was drinking the coffee, the phone rang.

"Sue, its Anna Marie. The Inn of the Ozarks was booked, no rooms were available. They suggested several hotels nearby. I would like to try the Joy Motel. I'll call you back."

I finished my cup of coffee and waited for Sue to call me. While waiting, I went back online to check on the history of the Ozark UFO Conference. I learned that the UFO Conference was created by the late Lou Farish. Lou was born in 1937 in Plumerville, Arkansas. In his teen years, he had developed a curiosity regarding unexplained phenomena, including UFOs. By the 1970s, he was attending national UFO network symposia and writing articles for UFO magazines and journals. He served as co-editor from 1977-1990 and became the editor in 1991 of the UFO News Clipping Service.

In 1988, Bill Pitts of Fort Smith, Arkansas held a UFO Conference in Eureka Springs, Arkansas. Lou decided that there was a need for an annual UFO Conference in that region of the country. From 1989 through 2009 he directed the conference. The typical attendance was between 400-600 guests. After twenty years, Lou stepped aside and turned the leadership over to Lee Clinton, who had managed the conference audio visual production for most of those years. In 2013, Lee passed the leadership to Delores Cannon. The conference was renamed the Ozark Mountain UFO Conference.

Delores spent forty-five years as a hypnotherapist and past life regressionist. She had written 19 books which were published by the Ozark Mountain Publishing Company, founded in 1992 by Delores and her husband, Johnny Cannon. The company only published non-fiction metaphysical and spiritual books.

The telephone rang as I was reading about the history of the UFO Conference. I picked up the phone and said, "Hi."

"Hi Sue, it's me, Anna Marie. The Joy Hotel had only one room left so I booked it. The room is non-smoking, two double beds, a television set, and a coffee machine."

"What's the cost?" I asked.

"Eighty dollars a night. The three days' cost will be $240, but of course, that doesn't include breakfast."

"That sounds like a good deal to me, Anna Marie. We won't have to worry about breakfast since we can drive right across the street to Myrtie Mae's Restaurant. I'll go ahead and register us for the conference. I'll talk to you later."

I called the number for the conference. A woman answered the phone.

"Are tickets still available for the UFO Conference?

"Yes, she said. "In the meeting room there are only a few seats left, one in the back of the room, and two on the far left side near the front."

"I will take the two seats on the left side. What is the cost for the three day conference?

"The cost is $150, which does not include meals. Please give me your name, address, e-mail address and credit card."

"My name is Sue Henry and my friend's name is Anna Marie. We live in Springfield, Missouri."

I gave her our addresses and my credit card. She said she would send me the registration confirmation through e-mail.

Immediately I called Anna Marie and shared the good news.

"How shall we prepare for the conference?" asked Anna Marie.

"Why don't we look for books and reference materials about UFOs? I would like to read one of Delores Cannon's books about past life regression. Since I have had a past life regression with a therapist in Springfield, I am interested in reading about Delores' work."

Curious to read one of Delores Cannon's books, I went online to the Amazon web page to order one. There were many books listed. I decided to order *The Convoluted Universe* and *Search for Hidden Sacred Knowledge*.

That evening at the dinner table, I discussed my interest in attending the UFO Conference next month with my husband. I shared the information about alien abduction from one of the writers in our group. He questioned the mental health of the person and said, "I don't believe in alien abduction, but I'll try to keep an open mind."

He was interested in reading the book I had ordered, but he was not interested in attending the UFO Conference. My husband and I are avid readers, and we like to share the books that we have read. However, we have different interests in subject matter. Primarily, he likes science, politics, history and some murder mysteries. I like novels, new age books, and mysteries. I like to write, but he doesn't. Someday he may start writing, and maybe we can co-write a novel. That would be fun.

Chapter Two

Six months before the UFO Conference, Alice Shaw, an attractive thirty year old female with blonde hair and blue eyes, drove to the city library to attend the Metaphysical group in Little Rock, Arkansas. She was excited to share the news that she would be making a presentation at the April UFO Conference. She wore a tailored navy blue pant suit and high heels. She had been a member of the group for a couple of years. She was introduced to the group by Anton Browning, a friend she met at a bar in downtown Little Rock.

There was a mutual attraction. Anton was 5 foot 11 inches, had dark curly hair, and a smile that swept her off her feet. She talked about her research work at the branch extension of the University of Arkansas. He told her that he was working in an antique store also in downtown Little Rock. He was fascinated with Alice's research work with cattle mutilation. He told her about the Metaphysical group and invited her to join.

"The group meets the first Wednesday evening of the month in a meeting room of the local library. I hope to see you at the next meeting."

Alice parked her car in the library parking lot. She quickly ran up the stairs to the library, excited about her good news.

As she entered the room, the meeting had just started. The leader of the group, Joe Weiss, introduced the new members. The older members said, "Welcome to the group."

"Before we begin the program for the evening, are there any announcements?" asked Joe.

"Yes, I would like to make an announcement," said Alice. "I have been asked to make a presentation on Sunday morning at the UFO Conference in April in Eureka Springs in Northwest Arkansas. My topic is *Cattle Mutilation*. Many of you know that I have been doing research for the University of Arkansas and have traveled all around the country gathering data on cattle mutilation. So far my data is inconclusive about the cause of the mutilation. Some people have linked it to aliens from

146

another planet coming to earth and experimenting with animals. The conference will cover many topics related to UFOs and aliens visiting earth. One of the keynote speakers will be Erich Von Daniken, who wrote *Chariots of the Gods*. His work has created a lot of interest in aliens coming to earth. The book has sold thousands of copies. Also, he has appeared on the television's History Channel. We may find him interesting.

The cost for the three day conference is only $150. Of course, the hotel room and meals would be extra. You can go on the web and download the information."

"That sounds like fun," said Clara Spencer, a tall middle-aged female, with brown hair and brown eyes. "I have never attended the conference. This year may be the time to go."

"I don't know if I can get away from work to attend the conference," said Arthur Spencer, Clara's husband. Arthur was several inches taller than Clara. He had black hair and black eyes. He was wearing a dark blue shirt over pressed blue jeans and brown loafers. His business partner, Mickey Slater, was sitting next to him.

Mickey said, "I think we can arrange it. Possibly, we might be able to do some business in Northwest Arkansas. We haven't tapped that market as yet."

Mickey was over 6 feet tall and weighed around 250 pounds. He was well dressed in designer clothes. He wore a Rolex watch around his right wrist and a large gold ring with a diamond on his left hand ring finger.

"I think it would be fun to attend the conference," said Sandra Taylor, sitting next to Mickey. Sandra was a slim, attractive female with bleached blonde hair, around 5 feet, 5 inches tall. She was dressed in designer clothes and wore expensive gold necklaces and gold bracelets around her left wrist. She and Mickey were close friends. They always arrived and left the meeting together.

"Where can we get the information to register?" asked Clara.

"You can go online to find the conference website," said Alice. She spelled out the website address to the group.

"Is there anyone else in the group that has an announcement?" asked Joe. "If not, I will introduce the speaker for the evening's program. Karl Setrum is from Little Rock and works at the library in the Research section. He will discuss the metaphysical theories of Theosophy."

For the next hour and half, the Metaphysical group listened to Karl discuss the theories of Theosophy. There was a 15 minute break during the presentation. Anton went to the restroom while other members took a coffee break.

While he was in a stall, Anton heard the door to the restroom open and footsteps enter. He immediately recognized the voices of Mickey and Arthur discussing their business.

"Are you sure that the gray sofa in the back room of our store has enough space in the frame to stash our goods?" said Mickey. Then he noticed Anton's shoes under one of the stalls.

He pushed on the door, but it was locked. "Anton! Come out. Do not repeat anything that I have said or you will be in big trouble."

Anton pulled up his trousers, flushed the toilet and opened the door. He looked at Mickey and said, "No, I won't repeat anything you said. Actually, I'm not sure I heard anything you said."

Anton washed his hands and left the restroom, leaving Mickey and Arthur in the restroom. Anton walked back to his chair and sat down. The speaker continued his presentation.

After the meeting, Anton suggested to Alice that they go to the pub across the street and discuss the UFO Conference. They walked out of the library, crossed the street, and entered the pub.

As they were sitting in a booth, Anton told Alice what had happened in the restroom.

"That is strange, I wonder what he meant by 'stashing goods in the sofa'?"

"I don't know, and I don't want to find out," said Anton.

They changed the subject and discussed the UFO conference.

Chapter Three

Since the registration for the conference started on a Friday morning at 8:00, we decided to drive to Eureka Springs the day before. Thursday morning I awoke early, ate breakfast, and took a short walk around the block. The sky was clear with a bright morning sun. The day will be perfect for driving, not like the icy roads the last time Anna Marie and I drove to Eureka Springs.

I had packed my clothes in a suitcase the night before so that I wouldn't have to rush the next day. I planned to pick up Anna Marie at 10:00 a.m. I put my suitcase into the trunk of my Honda Fit and drove to Anna Marie's house. I wore my best jeans, a blue shirt, and a sweater coat. She was waiting on her front porch for my arrival. She was wearing black jeans, a red sweater, and a black vest. The red sweater complemented her black hair. For a small woman, she had a very large suitcase. When she saw me she picked up her suitcase and rain coat and walked to my car. I stepped out of the car and helped her put her suitcase in the trunk. The suitcase was heavy. Both of us had to lift it into the trunk.

"Hi Anna Marie, how are you?"

"Hi Sue, I am so excited. The day is finally here."

"Yes, it is. Let's go."

For the next hour and a half we drove south on Interstate 65 to Mo 86, Exit 3. As we drove across the bridge over Table Rock Lake, I noticed white seagulls flying over and fishermen in their boats hoping to catch fish. What a pleasant day to drive.

The drive seemed short because we talked the whole time about the UFO books we had read and books by Delores Cannon.

As we passed Golden, Missouri, I said, "Have you ever stopped at the museum in Golden?"

"No, I haven't, have you?"

"Yes, my husband and I stopped one day. The museum is an amazing place. I particularly liked the gemstones and American Indian artifacts. I highly recommend it."

"Maybe," said Sue, "we can stop on the way back from Eureka Springs after the conference."

"Maybe, if we aren't too exhausted."

As we crossed the state line to Arkansas, we took Route 23 through Holiday Island. Holiday Island is like a suburb of Eureka Springs, five miles north of the village near Table Rock Lake. As I drove around a curve in the road, a deer ran across the road in front of me. Instinctively I put on the brakes. "Whew!" We almost had an accident."

"Wow!" said Anna Marie. "I am so glad you didn't hit the deer. That would have been tragic."

Both of us took deep breaths, and I resumed driving.

We arrived in Eureka Springs around 11:30 a.m. I parked the car in a parking lot near Basin Park. We decided to eat lunch at the Basin Park Hotel. Since the temperature was seventy-five degrees, the porch was open and we were able to sit outdoors.

Before sitting down I had stopped in the lobby and picked up some literature about the history of the hotel. While riding the elevator to the third floor, I read the information to Anna Marie.

In 2005 the Basin Park Hotel celebrated its 100-year anniversary on July 1. Located in the heart of this unique city, the historic hotel with its signature white limestone and pink dolomite rock walls is built into the side of the mountain on the north side of Basin Circle Park. The beautiful limestone exterior was quarried from the nearby town of Beaver. The hotel is adjacent to the cold water Basin Spring, which came to be the heart of the new health resort community 100 years ago.

During the 40s and 50s the Basin Park Hotel was a mecca for those who loved to party and gamble. Because the hotel is built into the side of a hill, every floor at the rear of the eight-story building is a ground floor. It is perfect for a quick escape if there is a fire, but in those days, it was said to be perfect for a quick escape from the law.

Marty and Elise Roenigk purchased the Basin Park Hotel in February 1987, and pledged to restore the hotel to its original grandeur. That pledge has become reality. Their multi-million dollar restoration and refurbishing of the hotel was recognized recently when they were presented the coveted Heritage Award at the Arkansas Governor's Conference.

Anna Marie said, "Thanks for reading that. There must have been some good times years ago in this hotel. If the hotel could talk, there would be many stories to tell."

As we approached the restaurant, a waitress showed us a place to sit and gave us menus. I was hungry and chose a salmon salad and coffee to drink. Anna Marie chose a fruit salad and tea. As we waited for our meal, we looked up and down the streets. People were milling about, walking in and out of shops.

"What a beautiful day to be in Eureka Springs," I said to Anna Marie. "Since we can't check into our hotel until 3:00, let's go shopping and visit the springs."

"Good idea," said Anna Marie. "I would like to take some photos of the flowers in bloom around the springs. We won't have time to go sight-seeing while we're at the conference." As we were talking about places to see, the waitress brought us our food. This salmon salad was as delicious as I had hoped. The dill sauce on the salmon added a zest to the dish.

After lunch we stopped at the Basin Park to listen to a guitar player. Musicians come to Eureka Springs to play and earn money. They put a hat on the sidewalk in front of them so tourists will give them money for playing. After 15 minutes of listening to the music, we started walking up the steep sidewalk of Spring Street. Primarily, we were window shopping until something caught our eyes, and we went inside the shop.

Around 2:45 we walked back down the street to my car and drove to the Joy Motel on upper Highway 62 West. While we registered for the room, Anna Marie picked up a flyer describing the motel. She read the flyer to me.

The Joy Motel is the area's only mid-century modern motel. It dates back to the 1950s and 60s. The hotel has been recently renovated with a mix of retro design and modern amenities. It is nestled under a canopy of native pines. There is a newly refinished chemical-free saltwater pool that is not open until June.

"The motel looks old, and, of course, it is; but now, I have a different attitude about the motel. It's a mid-century motel," I commented. "We'll have to check out the room to see if there is any mid-century furniture or artwork."

Our room was on the second floor overlooking the swimming pool and trees. We walked into our room and noticed a Lava lamp.

"Look, Anna Marie, a mid-century lamp. I hadn't seen one of those since the 60s."

We unpacked our clothes and hung them in a tiny closet. On our beds there was a note stating that *eco-friendly all natural fiber linens are used on the beds.* That sounds good to me.

"I'm tired, I would like to lie down for a while and rest."

"I agree," said Anna Marie.

We took off our shoes, pulled back the bedspread, and lay down. Soon I heard snoring. Anna Marie was asleep. I closed my eyes and soon fell asleep.

An hour later, we awoke. Anna Marie wanted to take a shower. I decided to read the *Eureka Springs Visitor Guide* that was on a table in the room. It was printed by the Greater Eureka Springs Chamber of Commerce. The Guide had everything a person would need to know about Eureka Springs.

Two articles caught my eye. The first one was *Shopper's Paradise*. The article said that there are over 150 specialty shops with no big box stores or outlet malls in Eureka Springs. *The crown jewel of shopping has been the talented artists and crafters available in over 20 galleries.*

I like jewelry and I like art. We will have to take some time out to visit these shops.

At 2:30 some of the members of the Little Rock Metaphysical group arrived in Eureka Springs. Alice Shaw was the only member to have a room at the Best Western Inn of the Ozarks. Because she was a presenter, a room had been reserved for her. She had been riding with Anton Browning. He drove to the Inn and dropped her off at the front door to check in. He waited in his car until she came back outdoors.

She said, "My room is around at the back of the Inn." She stepped back into the car and Anton drove around to the back of the Inn. As she got out, Anton opened the trunk and picked up her suitcase and carried it to her room.

"Goodbye, I'll see you later," said Anton as he bent down to kiss her.

She returned the kiss and said, "I'll see you later."

Anton drove off to Swiss Village Inn, a couple of blocks from the Best Western Inn of the Ozarks. As he pulled up to the inn, he saw Mickey Slater and Sandra Taylor unloading suitcases from Mickey's Jaguar in front of the inn. There was a U-Haul trailer hooked to the Jaguar. Anton parked his car near the office of the inn. He stepped out of his car and walked over to see Mickey and Sandra.

Anton said, "Hi. How was the trip?"

"Long and boring," said Mickey.

"Finally, we have arrived," said Sandra.

"It looks like you have hauled some furniture with you. Do you have a buyer in Eureka Springs?"

"Close by, he lives near Beaver Lake," replied Sandra.

"I hope your sale is successful. I'll see you later, I have to check in," said Anton.

"Why did you tell Anton that the buyer was from Beaver Lake?" said Mickey to Sandra."

"I didn't want him to become more suspicious. He knows too much."

Mickey and Sandra walked to their hotel room and locked the door.

"How do we locate the buyer? Do you have his phone number?" asked Sandra.

"Yes, I do. Don't worry about him contacting us; he's one of the speakers at the UFO Conference and can't meet us until after the conference."

"Okay, I'll trust you to make the contact," said Sandra.

Around the same time Arthur and Clara checked into the Joy Motel. Their room was on the ground floor overlooking the swimming pool. "I wish the weather was warmer. I would like to go for a swim," said Arthur.

"I am exhausted from the long trip. I want to take a shower and a nap," said Clara.

"Good idea," said Arthur.

Later that evening, they ate dinner at Rogue's Manor, an upscale and rather expensive restaurant, next door to Sweet Spring, one of many springs and gardens maintained by the Parks and Recreation Commission.

At 6:00 pm Anna Marie and I decided to find a place to eat. After looking at the list of restaurants in the Visitor Guide, we chose KJ's Caribe Restaurant and Cantina. The literature stated that it is a Mexican and Caribbean restaurant located on 62 West. They are known for using fresh local products in the dishes.

When we arrived at the restaurant the parking lot had only a few spaces left. The building was painted red with a painted picture of a Madonna or goddess. Flowers and grasses were growing all around the restaurant. It looked like a home. There were only eight tables inside the restaurant, but we only had to wait for a few minutes until one was ready. We both ordered margaritas and looked over the menu. I ordered scallops on a chalupa and Anna Marie ordered a beef burrito. Rice and beans came with the main course. The food was delicious, and the margaritas were outstanding.

After dinner we drove around Eureka Springs, pausing by each spring to look at the flowers. On the way home we stopped at Brews, a small pub on Spring Street. It appeared to be a local spot located next door to the Fine Art Gallery. We parked near Sweet Spring and walked to the pub.

The Pub was crowded. We found a place near the front window. I went to the bar to place our order of two beers. At the table next to us sat two couples. There were two men, one younger than the other by at least 15 years. The woman sitting next to the older man was wearing a wedding ring and seemed about 10 years younger than the older man. The other woman didn't have a wedding ring and looked to be in her thirties. We overheard them talking about the UFO Conference, so we introduced ourselves to them.

"Pardon me, my name is Sue Henry and this is Anna Marie. I couldn't help overhearing you talking about the UFO Conference. We also plan to attend the conference tomorrow. We're from Springfield, Missouri."

"Hi," replied the older man. "My name is Arthur Spencer. This is my wife, Clara Spencer."

Next, the younger man said, "My name is Anton Browning."

His partner spoke, "My name is Alice Shaw." We are all from Little Rock. I am one of the speakers on Sunday morning. I'll be talking about *Cattle Mutilation*. I have been traveling all over the United States visiting the sites of mutilation. I will report on my research."

Clara interrupted Alice by saying, "We belong to a Metaphysical group. This the first time we have attended a UFO Conference. Several years ago Delores Cannon came to Little Rock to talk about regression therapy and help us discover our past lives. She told us that groups of people seem to reincarnate together. It seems that our group in Little Rock has reincarnated together. Some of us were the opposite sex; some of us were married to another person in the group; others were parents. It seems so complicated. For instance, in my recent past life I was married to Anton."

"I find that awkward," said Arthur. But, we remain good friends."

"It's like we are family, related emotionally, not genetically," said Anton.

"I can see where that can lead to complicated relationships," I said."

I was beginning to feel uncomfortable about their personal relationships. I decided to change the subject. "We're staying at the Joy Motel. There are so many people attending this conference that we couldn't get a room at the conference hotel, the Best Western Inn of the Ozarks.

Arthur spoke, "Clara and I are also staying at the Joy Motel. Maybe we will see you there."

Anton spoke up, "I am staying at the Swiss Village Inn."

"I am staying at the Best Western Inn of the Ozarks," said Alice. "They had a difficult time finding a place to stay. The Inn of the Ozarks was booked over a year ago when the conference was announced," said Alice.

We finished our beers and said, "Good-by, enjoy the conference."

As we were leaving a man and woman asked if they could have our seats.

"Yes, you can. We were just leaving."

As I opened the door to leave I overheard the couple greeting the foursome saying, "We finally found you."

I drove back to our motel around 10:00. I was tired, ready to go to sleep.

Anna Marie said, "I had such a good nap, I'm going to read before going to sleep. Will my light bother you?"

"No, I'll face the other direction. Good-night."

"Good-night."

Chapter Four

On the day of the conference we awoke at 7:00. Quickly we dressed and drove to Myrtie Mae's Restaurant at the Inn of the Ozarks for breakfast. As we sat down, a waitress asked if we wanted coffee. Immediately I said "Yes." After she brought our coffees, she asked what we wanted to eat.

"I'll have two scrambled eggs with cheese." Anna Marie said, "I will have a waffle."

When the food arrived, we leisurely ate our breakfast. We had plenty time to register. Although registration was open at 8:00, the conference didn't start until 11:15.

The Conference Center was located in a large building in back of the Best Western Inn of the Ozarks. The parking lot was almost full. We found a space at the back of the lot. We arrived at 8:15. The registration line was long, and we had to wait 10 minutes before receiving our registration materials. As we were waiting in line I looked all around the room.

"Look, Anna Marie, do you see that gray alien standing near the restrooms?"

"Yes, it looks so real. I want a photo of me next to the alien. That will be proof that I attended this conference."

Vendors were everywhere, upstairs and downstairs. After registration we visited the vendors. First, we looked at the bookstore of Ozark Mountain Publishing Company founded by the Cannons. There were so many books on spirituality, self-help, new age, meditation, dowsing, healing, metaphysics, and books by Delores Cannon. Next, we looked at jewelry at a New Age Crystal booth. As I looked around the room, I saw booths with Tarot readings, psychic readings, CDs, etc. Everything you can imagine about spirituality, new age, crop circles, and UFOs was present.

We walked around until 10:30. Then, we went inside the meeting room and found our seats. We were told that over nine hundred people had registered for the conference.

Before the program started, I looked around the room to see if I recognized anyone. I noticed that Arthur and Clara Spencer, the couple that we met last night at the pub, were sitting near the back of the room. The other couple, Anton and Alice, was sitting in the middle of the room.

The first session opened at 11:15. A welcome was given by the Director of the conference. The first speaker spoke on *Crop Circles* from 11:30 to 1:00 p.m. Crop circles were defined by the speaker *as a pattern created by flattening a crop.* Aerial photo views of crop circles from many countries were shown. The speaker said that the number of crop circles has substantially increased from the 1970s to current times. Many theories were postulated as to the cause of crop circles. The most popular theory is that aliens created the crop circles. Since I had seen a crop circle near Avebury, England ten years ago, I thought that it was impossible for someone to create such an accurate depiction of circles unless precise machines were used.

By the time the presentation was over, we were starving. The break was only thirty minutes. Lunch consisted of sandwiches and beverages that were sold in the lobby. We didn't have much time to eat, drink, and use the restroom, but we made it back in time for the next speaker at 1:30. There were two other speakers in the afternoon with topics of *UFO Sightings,* followed by a two hour dinner break. The presentation was informative, but I was tired of sitting. I needed to stand up and stretch.

For dinner we decided to eat at the Thai restaurant. To our surprise we saw the older couple, Arthur and Clara Spencer sitting in the far corner of the restaurant. They did not seem too happy. Their voices were escalating. People in the restaurant were staring at them. Suddenly, Clara started crying and rushed out of the restaurant. Arthur paid the bill and ran after her.

"I wonder what that was all about," I said.

"I'm sorry to see them fight. They seemed to be such a nice couple," said Anna Marie.

After dinner we drove back to the conference.

Arthur and Clara walked to their car. Arthur unlocked the doors and opened the door for Clara. Clara sat down in the car and said, "I am not in love with Anton," as she wiped the tears from her eyes. "Even though we were a couple in a past life, that does not mean I am in love with him today."

Arthur responded, "I can see the way you look at him; you are in love with him. Tell me the truth!" He grabbed her arm.

"Leave me alone. You have to trust me."

Arthur started the motor and drove to their motel.

The evening session had one speaker who showed a video and spoke for two hours about *Alien Abductions*. After his talk, two men dressed as gray aliens grabbed the speaker and left the room. "What was that all about?" I asked Anna Marie. Other people in the audience were also talking and wondering what happened. "Should we call the police or 911?"

The director of the conference walked to the microphone saying, "Don't worry, the two aliens were humans dressed as aliens to offer some humor during the conference. Our speaker is okay."

The audience laughed. The meeting was over and people moved to the cash bar.

Anna Marie and I stayed for drinks and mingled with the other attendees. It seemed that most people knew each other since people were greeting each other with hugs.

At 11:15 we arrived back at our motel. We heard police sirens and saw an emergency vehicle drive into the motel parking lot. We followed the vehicle and parked the car. Two men from the emergency vehicle ran to the swimming pool. A man, wearing street clothes, was floating in the pool face down. Since the pool was only a couple of feet deep, the EMTs waded into the pool and brought the man out. The manager was standing by the pool.

Anna Marie and I looked at each other. She looked shocked, and I felt the same emotion. I didn't want to look at the body. Yet, I was curious. We stepped out of the car and walked to where the manager was standing.

"What happened?" I asked.

"I don't know. I was ready to go home when I noticed the man in the pool and called 911."

"Who is this man?"

"I don't recognize him. He is not checked in at the motel."

Just then, the Sheriff's car arrived. The Sheriff and Deputy stepped out of their car and walked over to the EMTs.

"Is the man dead?"

"Yes. We tried resuscitating him, but now we need the Coroner to verify this man's death. He had a bruise around his neck. Possibly, he was strangled with a wire."

"Have you checked his pockets for identification?"

"Yes, he had a wallet in an inside pocket. Here it is."

The Sheriff looked through the wallet for identification. He found a Driver's License with the name of Anton Browning, age thirty-two, white, with a Little Rock address."

He walked over to the manager, and said,

"Are you the manager? Can you tell me what happened?"

"I was leaving the motel for the night when I noticed a body in the pool. The pool is not open for guests since the water and air are too cold. I walked to the pool to see who was swimming. I saw the man floating in the water; he was not moving. I called 911."

"Thanks for the information. I want to interview all your guests. Maybe someone knows the man and can give us some information. Please give me the register," said the Sheriff.

As the manager walked back into the motel office to pick up the register, I approached the Sheriff and said, "My name is Sue Henry. My friend, Anna Marie and I met Anton Browning at Brews last night. He was with a couple who said they were registered at this motel. They are Arthur and Clara Spencer. They said that they were from Little Rock."

"Thanks for the information," said the Sheriff. He walked away towards the motel office.

The manager opened the book to the past couple days for the Sheriff to see who was staying at the motel.

"May I have a copy of these names?" asked the Sheriff.

"Yes, I have a copy machine in the corner, and will run off a copy," said the manager.

"Please put up a notice in the motel that no one may leave the motel until the Sheriff has talked to each person."

"Yes, Sheriff, I will post a notice. "

"I'll be back here at 8:00 a.m. to begin interviewing the people registered at the motel."

Anna Marie and I heard the Sheriff telling the manager that all residents of the motel will be interviewed tomorrow. I walked to where the Sheriff was standing and asked to speak to him.

"Since Anna Marie and I gave you our statements tonight, we would like to attend the UFO Conference tomorrow instead of staying at the motel for your interviews. You can always reach us at the conference if you have any more questions."

"Yes, that would be fine. I appreciate your statements tonight. If I have any more questions, I know where to find you. May I have your cell phone number?"

I gave him the number of my cell phone.

"Thanks, Sue."

Anna Marie and I walked to our motel room. We climbed the stairs slowly, tired from all the excitement."

"I can't believe that Anton is dead. Was he murdered?

"I'm curious about why he was at this motel? He wasn't staying here," said Anna Marie.

"I think we are in the midst of a murder mystery," I said. "However, I am exhausted and ready to go to sleep."

I undressed, put on my night clothes, turned off the light, and went to bed. Anna Marie also went to bed. However, I had a difficult time sleeping. I turned and tossed while thinking about the murder. Finally, around

1:00 a.m. I fell asleep. That night I had nightmares of being chased by a man with a knife. I did not have a restful sleep.

Chapter Five

The second day of the conference started at 8:45. Anna Marie and I had slept until 8:00. We quickly dressed and rushed over to Myrtie Mae's for coffee and a muffin. Then we drove to the conference. No parking spaces were available. We had to park near the restaurant and walk a block to the conference.

The first speaker of the day was a U.S. Air Force veteran who believes a UFO incident that he experienced while he was on duty in 1980 is the root of his current health problems. Initially the government denied he was on active duty at the time. With the help of a lawyer and a U.S. senator his records have been corrected, and he has received his full medical disability.

In 1980 he was serving as a U.S. Air Force police officer at Royal Air Force Base (RAF) Bentwaters, near the

172

Rendelsham Forest in Suffolk in the United Kingdom. It was December when the UFO incident took place. The base was on lease to the U.S. He described the incident in detail. Quickly I wrote down his comments as he was speaking.

Late on the night of the fateful incident, lights were seen in the forest and I and several other security personnel were sent out to investigate. We saw a bright light that grew brighter as they approached. It then flew off into the night sky. The next night the lights were seen again. Skeptical of the whole affair, and eager to figure out what he assumed was a prosaic answer to the sightings; the Commander took a group of us men out again. This time, the entire group saw lights flying around the forest. Some of these orbs of light beamed rays of light on the ground near the men's feet and on the nearby munitions storage. The event became a large story in the UK, and is still debated to this day. I approached closest to the object. I feel that my health issues stem from my proximity to the UFO. I was exposed to radiation for longer than normal.

Since that time I have suffered from congestive heart failure, which I have been told by scientists can be caused by radiation exposure.

The audience was very quiet during the time he was telling his story. When he was through, the audience clapped for a long time. Here was a story about a man fighting the government for his right for medical disability and winning. During the thirty minute break between speakers I received a phone call from the Sheriff asking Anna Marie and me to come to the motel.

"Yes, we will be there in 15 minutes." I shared the information with Anna Marie.

"Oh no, we'll miss hearing the other morning speaker," said Anna Marie.

We left the conference and walked up the hill to my car. I drove to the Joy Motel and parked in the parking lot. I saw a group of the residents sitting outdoors in chairs with the Sheriff talking to them. We left the car and joined the group.

"Thanks for coming," the Sheriff said when he saw us.

Anna Marie and I found a couple chairs and sat down, anxious to hear what the Sheriff had to say.

"The Coroner confirmed to us that the body found in the pool was Anton Browning and that he had been murdered. He was killed with a wire placed around his neck, strangling him and was dead before being put into the pool. Also, there was alcohol in his stomach. Someone wanted the murder to look like an accident. It appears Anton Browning was murdered around 9:30 p.m. and was dragged into the pool. At first we all thought it was an accident that Anton had been drinking and had fallen into the pool. Did anyone hear or witness any arguments last night?" asked the Sheriff.

The residents looked at one another shaking their heads. "No," everyone replied.

I looked around at the group. I did not see Arthur and Clara Spencer. Anton seemed to be their good friend. I thought they might have something to say that would add to the investigation and wondered where they were.

After little response from the residents, the Sheriff said, "You can all go to your rooms, but do not leave the motel until I give you permission."

After the residents left I approached the Sheriff and said, "Anna Marie and I might have more information to give to you. It may not be useful, but we will share what we know."

"Please sit down and share what you know or think."

"Last night Anna Marie and I ate dinner at the Thai restaurant. We saw Arthur and Clara at the restaurant. They seemed to be arguing since their voices were loud. Clara then began to cry and ran out of the restaurant. Her husband followed her. At first, we felt that it was none of our business to see a couple fighting.

"But then, we remembered our conversations with them the night before. They were talking about past life regression and reincarnation. They said that Anton was the husband of Clara in a previous lifetime. Do you think it might be possible that Arthur was jealous and killed Anton? "

I was still wondering where they were this morning.

"That is quite a story. I'm not sure I believe in reincarnation, but if Arthur and Clara believe it, it could be a motive for murder."

"Where are they? I did not see them among the residents. They told us that they were staying at this motel." I asked.

"They didn't show up for our meeting this morning. We checked their room, and their bed had been slept in. They must have left early this morning before our arrival. I don't know where they are," said the Sheriff. He turned to his Deputy and said, "Send out a report to all policemen that we are searching for a missing couple." The Sheriff shared the descriptive details of the couple with the Deputy.

"Hopefully we will find them," said the Sheriff.

"Can we go back to the UFO Conference?" I asked.

"Yes, you can. I'll call you if I need you."

Since we missed the second morning speaker, we went to lunch at Myrtie Mae's. Following lunch we attend the afternoon session, which started at 1:30.

The speaker for the first afternoon session was a woman from California. She was introduced as a Certified Hypnotherapist and Regression Therapist, researcher, and writer. Her topic was, *Case Studies of ET Experiencers*. Before sharing case studies, she said that in 1991 she began working with people who had encounters with extraterrestrial beings. She has counseled and conducted regressions with more than fourteen thousand of these people, which resulted in at least three thousand regressions. Twenty-five of these cases are included in her book, *Alien Experiences*, a collaborative work with another writer and illustrator. Besides sharing some of these case studies, she shared her experiences as a Crop Circle researcher since 1990. She researches and conducts tours to crop circles in England each summer. She co-authored the book, *Crop Circles Revealed: Language of the Light Symbol*, in 2001.

I found the case studies fascinating, and had no idea that so many people have reported encounters with extraterrestrial beings. I think I will purchase her book on *Alien Experiences* to learn more about these events.

During break time at 3:00, as Anna Marie and I walked back to the vendors, I saw Alice Shaw. I waved to her and indicated I wanted to talk to her.

"Hi Alice, do you have a few minutes to talk?"

"I only have a few minutes. I have an appointment to talk to a reporter from one of the local newspapers about my presentation tomorrow."

"Did you hear about Anton Browning's accident?"

"No, I haven't! What happened! Is he okay?"

"He was found in the swimming pool at the Joy Motel

177

with his face down in the water last night. The Sheriff said he was murdered."

"That can't be true. I had dinner with him last night." She paused, wiped her eyes, blew her nose, and continued talking. "I feel terrible, we were such good friends. After dinner he took me to my room at the inn. I invited him in for a drink. He said he would like to, but he couldn't. He had received a note from Mickey last night when all of us were at Brews. The note said for Anton to meet him at the Historical Museum's parking lot at 9:00. He was to come alone. I'm sorry, but I can't talk any longer. I have to run and meet with the reporter."

"When you have time, talk to the Sheriff with your information."

"I will thanks."

Anna Marie and I looked at each. She said, "Did Mickey kill Anton? How do we find out? The Sheriff needs to have that information.

"We can't do anything now. Alice will have to convey that information."

We decided to look at the vendors and then attend the program after the break. First, I went to the Ozark Mountain Publishing booth. I purchased *Alien Experiences*. Anna Marie looked at a vendor selling jewelry. She purchased a clear crystal that was found in

Southwest Arkansas. It was mounted on a silver chain. She decided to wear it. She opened the clasp and put it around her neck.

"Isn't this quartz beautiful? It will give me positive vibrations."

"Yes, it is beautiful."

As we were walking towards the meeting room, my cell phone rang. The Sheriff was calling.

"Sue, I need you and Anna Marie to identify two bodies we found when their car ran off a steep road on Highway 62 West."

"Why do you want us? We know very few people in Eureka Springs."

"You may know this couple. They were staying at the Joy Motel."

"Give me the directions and we will be there." The Sheriff gave me the directions, and I shared the information with Anna Marie.

Minutes later I was driving my car on Highway 62 West with Anna Maria sitting next to me. We drove several miles, passing the sign for Thorncrown Chapel, until we saw flashing lights on several police cars parked on the right side of the road. I parked my car behind the last car. As we stepped out of the car, the Sheriff, standing on the other side of the highway, saw us and waved his hand for

179

us to come where he was standing. As we approached him we saw two black body bags on the side of the road.

"I want you to identify this couple," said the Sheriff as he zipped open first one bag, then the other one. I gasped. Although there was blood on their foreheads, I still recognized them.

"Yes, I can identify this couple. We met them at Brews on Friday night. They were friends with Anton Browning."

Anna Marie also acknowledged that she had recognized the couple.

"It looks like they were driving too fast on a curve and drove over the edge," said the Sheriff.

"Do you think it was an accident?"

"No, it was murder. The brake line was severed, and the driver was unable to stop the car. We have no idea who murdered this couple," said the Sheriff.

"I don't know who the murderer is, but I think the fourth member of the two couples may need protection. Her name is Alice Shaw. She was a good friend of Anton. Have you contacted her?"

"Not yet, we don't have her phone number or the place where she is staying."

"We saw her about thirty minutes ago at the conference. She had dinner with Anton last night. We don't have her phone number. You might want to contact the UFO

Conference registrar for her phone number since she was attending the conference and is a speaker on Sunday morning."

"Good idea," said the Sheriff.

"Can we leave or do you still need us?"

"You may go. I know how to reach you if I need to."

As we walked back to the car, I said to Anna Marie,

"Let's stop at Thorncrown Chapel since it is only a mile back on the highway. Maybe by visiting the Chapel we can think of other things besides the murder."

"That's a good idea. The photo of the Chapel on the advertisement is beautiful. Let's go," said Anna Marie.

As we drove into the parking lot, I felt a sense of awe when I saw Thorncrown Chapel. Anna Marie picked up a flyer that was on a bench at the entrance of the chapel. She read to flyer to me:

The chapel is 48 feet tall with 425 windows and over 6,000 square feet of glass. All this glass sits atop one hundred tons of native stone and colored flagstone. Thorncrown Chapel was the winner of the American Institute of Architecture's Design of the Year Award for 1981 and the AIA Design of the Decade Award for the 1980's."

"That's impressive," I said.

We walked through the door and sat in one of the pews. The silence of the chapel helped to soothe our emotions and thoughts. Ten minutes later we heard a voice saying,

"Visitor hours are over. I must lock the door."

I stood up and turned around to see a young man standing by the door.

"What a beautiful and serene chapel," I said to him.

"Yes, many people who visit the chapel say the same things. I feel fortunate to be the caretaker."

As we drove away from Thorncrown Chapel, I said, "Where shall we eat dinner? I would like to go to a quiet place."

"Let me look in our information packet to see if any restaurants are listed," said Anna Marie. We opened the car doors and sat down. Anna Marie picked up the information packet and looked for restaurants.

"The Cottage Inn Restaurant is a possibility, it is on this highway. We passed it on the way out here; it is three miles east of Thorncrown Chapel."

"It sounds good to me. Will you call them to see if we can get a reservation?"

"Yes, I will." Anna Marie called the restaurant. She was told that we could have a reservation at 5:30. It was now 5:15; we would be able to arrive in time for dinner. As we were driving to the Cottage Inn Restaurant, Anna read the advertisement to me.

The Cottage Inn Restaurant & Lodging, is located on the 'Quiet Side' of Eureka Springs, offers the exciting flavors of the Mediterranean. Enjoy the country setting, delicious cuisine, and the peacefulness of the Ozarks. The restaurant chef-owner has studied and traveled throughout Europe and her passion for the Mediterranean is reflected in the menu of her restaurant.

"Just what we need," I said to Anna Marie. They have good food and a quiet place to eat.

Ten minutes later we arrived at the Cottage Inn Restaurant. The outside of the restaurant was not impressive. Inside was a different story. All the tables had white linen table cloths with a lighted candle. We were given a table by the window. The view of the woods had large pine trees and cedar trees. The waitress asked for our drink order. I ordered a glass of Merlot and Anna Marie asked for Chablis. While waiting for our drinks, we looked over the menu. There was a special tonight that looked appetizing. They were serving fresh rainbow trout with truffles and asparagus. Both of us decided that we would order the special. When the waitress came back she asked for our order. She said that soup or salad came with the meal. I ordered a small salad and Anna Marie ordered the soup.

After the savory dinner we felt that the Cottage Inn lived up to its reputation. The meal was delicious; and the quiet ambience was what we needed. As we left the restaurant we realized that we had time to hear the keynote speaker at

7:00. The speaker was Erich von Daniken. I had read his book, *Chariots of the* Gods, and thought he had some good theories about extraterrestrial influences on early human culture. I drove to the conference and arrived five minutes before 7:00.

Erich von Daniken was introduced as the Swiss author of the best-selling book and television show, *Chariots of the Gods,* published in 1968. He is one of the main figures responsible for popularizing the *paleo-contact* and ancient astronaut's hypotheses. He became the co-founder of the Archaeology, Astronautics and SETI Research Association, and he designed Mystery Park, now known as Jungfrau Park, a theme park located in Interlaken, Switzerland, that opened in May 2003.

Erich von Daniken walked to the podium and began talking with a thick accent. I have paraphrased what he said.

Thank you for the introduction. Next week I will be 81 years old on April 14. I was born in 1935, in Zofingen, Aargau, Switzerland. I was brought up as a Roman Catholic and attended the Saint-Michel International Catholic School in Fribourg, Switzerland. During this time at school I rejected the church's interpretations of the Bible and developed an interest in astronomy and the phenomenon of flying saucers. At age 19 I left the school and was apprenticed to a Swiss hotelier for a time, before moving to Egypt. In December 1964 I wrote an article, Did Our Ancestors Have a Visit from Space? For the

German-Canadian periodical, Der Nordwesen. I returned to Switzerland and became manager of the Hotel Rosenhugel in Davos, Switzerland, during which time I wrote Chariots of the Gods.

I worked on the manuscript late at night after the hotel's guests had retired. The draft of the book was turned down by a variety of publishers. One publisher was willing to publish the book after a rewriting. The book was accepted for publication early in1967, but not printed until March 1968. Against all expectations, the book gained widespread interest and became a bestseller. I also wrote a second book, Gods from Outer Space.

I believe that extraterrestrials or "ancient astronauts" visited Earth and influenced early human culture. Such structures as the Egyptian pyramids, Stonehenge, and the Moai of Easter Island and artifacts from that period represent higher technological knowledge than is presumed to have existed at the times they were manufactured. I have also discovered ancient artwork throughout the world containing depictions of astronauts, air and space vehicles, extraterrestrials, and complex technology.

I will show slides of these examples of ancient astronauts who had visited earth and influenced the culture of Earth.

Lights were turned off and slides appeared on the screen. As I looked at the slides and heard von Daniken's interpretations, I was aware of how convincing he seemed to be. Yet, I was still a skeptic. Some of the criticism of von Daniken's books that I read several years ago, point out that prior to his work, other authors had presented ideas of extraterrestrial contacts. He had failed to credit these authors properly or at all, even when making the same claims, using similar or identical evidence. Other writers during the 1970s wrote books refuting von Daniken's theories.

However, von Daniken's theories are still popular. He is an occasional presenter on the History Channel and Ancient *Aliens,* where he talks about aspects of his theories as they pertain to each episode.

After von Daniken's presentation, he asked if there were any questions. Many people raised their hands and questioned some of his statements.

I found the presentation entertaining. Many questions and statements were raised with little to no evidence to support them, however.

After the meeting we joined other people at the cash bar that was open in the lobby. I had my usual glass of Merlot and Anna Marie drank a white wine. We walked around the room looking for anyone that we had met before. Off in a corner, I saw the couple that took our seats at Brews on Friday night. The man was over 6 feet tall and weighted around 250 pounds. He looked like a football player. The woman was average height, 5 foot 5 inches. She was slim and attractive with bleached blonde hair and blue eyes.

Both were wearing expensive clothes and jewelry. We joined them and introduced ourselves.

"Hi, my name is Sue Henry, and this is Anna Marie. We are from Springfield, Missouri. Do you remember us from giving you our seats at Brews?"

"Yes," said the man. "My name is Mickey Slater."

"My name is Sandra Taylor. So nice to meet you."

"Are you enjoying the conference?" I asked.

"Yes, we are," said Sandra, and Mickey nodded his head.

"Have you heard what happened to Arthur and Clara Spencer?" I asked.

"No, we haven't seen them at the conference today," replied Mickey.

"They were in a car accident on Highway 62 West and died when their car overturned," I said.

"What a shock!" replied Sandra. "That is such a tragedy. We were going to meet them for dinner tonight, but they didn't arrive. I wondered what had happened."

"The Sheriff asked Anne Marie and me to identify the bodies because we were the only ones at the motel where they were staying who could recognize them."

"That must have been an unpleasant experience," said Sandra."

"How true, it was not a pleasant sight. How long did you know the couple?" I asked.

"We knew them in Little Rock. All of us were in a Metaphysical group to explore psychic phenomenon and past lives. We discovered that many of us were related in a past life," replied Sandra.

"How interesting," I said. "Were you good friends?"

"Well," said Mickey. Arthur and I were in business together. I guess that makes us friends."

"What kind of business?" I asked.

"Imports and Exports. We sold antiques from various countries," said Mickey. "By the way, it is getting late and I am tired. I am ready to go back to our hotel."

"Are you staying at the Inn of the Ozarks?" I asked.

"No." replied Sandra.

"We are staying at the Joy Motel because we registered late." I said, "We will see you tomorrow. Good-night."

As we were walking to the car, Anna Marie said,

"I was uncomfortable talking to them. They seemed to look down on us, as if we were from the other side of the tracks."

"I had the same feeling. Did you notice that they gave us only short answers whenever I asked a question?"

"Yes, they seemed secretive."

"Let's go to our room and go to sleep. It has been a long day," I said. I drove my car to the Joy Motel. That night I slept well. I had no nightmares.

Chapter Six

Today is Sunday morning, the last day of the conference. I am so confused and have mixed feelings. It seems like I am watching a murder mystery novel of Agatha Christie's, *The Ten Little Indians*. Every day someone is killed. Who is next? I hope Alice Shaw is okay. The conference program says she is speaking at 9:00 am. Anna Marie and I are sitting in the meeting room waiting for the conference to start.

The lights go out and the director of the conference walks to the podium and speaks.

"Welcome, we have heard some great speakers this weekend. Now, however, I am sorry to announce that our first speaker today, Alice Shaw, will not be making her presentation. She received a message that there was an emergency with a family member in Little Rock, and she had to cancel her presentation. In her place, we will have a panel presentation."

Anna Marie and I were shocked and concerned.

"Did she really have an emergency?" I said.

"I hope she is not the latest victim," said Anna Marie.

"I think we should look for clues," I said. "Let's go to the Historical Muscum's parking lot and see if we can find anything."

"Why do we want to go there?" asked Anna Marie.

"Don't you remember what Clara said about Anton receiving a note to meet Mickey Slater at the museum's parking lot?" I said.

"Shouldn't we call the Sheriff first and tell him Clara is missing?"

"You can call him in the car while I am driving to the museum."

We left the conference, and I drove to the Museum.

When we arrived at the Museum, I parked my car in the parking lot. Since it was Sunday morning, it was empty. We stepped out of the car and looked around. We didn't find anything on the parking lot except for cigarette butts. I looked in the flower bed by the driveway.

"Look, Anna Marie, "I found something. It's a torn advertisement for Lake Leatherwood Park. It's located on 62 west a couple of miles west of Thorncrown Chapel. I think we should go there and look around. Whoever killed Anton might have taken Alice there."

"I agree," said Anna Marie. "Let's get back into the car and drive out there."

"While I'm driving, call the Sheriff and tell him what we found at the museum. Also, that we are driving to the park and looking around."

"Okay, I will do it," said Anna Marie.

"The Spencers were killed on the highway near Lake Leatherwood," I said. "The brakes might have been tampered with while they were at Lake Leatherwood. When they were driving back to Eureka Springs, the brakes gave out. What is going on at Lake Leatherwood?"

The drive to Lake Leatherwood was beautiful. The dogwood and redbud trees were in full bloom. Native flowers were blooming all along the highway. We drove to the parking lot. We parked and stepped out of the car. The lot was almost full. The camp area was full of tents and trailers. We walked around the parking lot looking for a suspicious car or truck. There were so many vehicles that I thought we were looking for a needle in a haystack. Suddenly, I stopped.

"Anna Marie, come here. Do you see what I see parked close to the woods?"

"It's a Jaguar. It seems out of place with these other cars and trucks. Let's walk over and take a close look," said Anna Marie.

The license tag was smeared with mud. I wiped the mud off. The license tag was issued in Little Rock.

"Anna Marie, look at the license tag. All of the victims were from Little Rock. "Let's look inside the car," I said.

We tried opening the doors but they were locked. Suddenly, we heard a thumping noise coming from the trunk.

"Is anyone in the trunk?" More thumping noise was heard.

"Who is in the trunk?" I asked Anna Marie. She shrugged her shoulders.

"Wait here, I'll walk over to the Lake Leatherwood office and see if anyone there can help us unlock the trunk." As I was walking toward the office I saw Mickey Slater walking down a path towards the Jaguar. I hid behind a tree and watched. He saw Anna Marie sitting down on a stump near the car.

"What are you doing here?" he asked. He grabbed her by the arm.

"Ouch, that hurts. I was tired from hiking around and looked for a place to sit."

"I don't believe you. Where's your friend?"

"She is getting coffee at the concession stand."

"Call her on your cell phone and ask her to come to the car, and tell her that you have found something you want to show her."

When I saw Anna Marie picking up her phone to call me, I quickly turned off my phone so Mickey couldn't hear my phone ring; otherwise, he would know that I was close by.

They waited for my response.

"Call her again. This time, call the right number!" He tightened his hold on her arm.

"Ouch, let go! That really hurts!"

"I am serious. Call your friend!"

Off in the distance I saw the Sheriff's car. He didn't have the car's siren on, so he was able to approach the parking lot without being seen. I backed away from my hiding place and slowly walked toward the Sheriff's car. He and his Deputy stepped out of the car and were ready to slam the door until they saw me. I held my finger to my lips, motioning them to be quiet. We slowly walked toward the Jaguar.

"I will distract the owner of the car so you can sneak up on him," I said to the Sheriff. The Sheriff looked at the Deputy, pointing at the trees, suggesting to him to walk through the trees around to the other side of the car.

Boldly, I walked toward the car and pretended that we were meeting old friends.

"Hi there—nice to see you again. Is everything okay?"

Mickey grabbed my arm and said, "Both of you are in trouble. You're spying on me. I know what to do with spies!"

Just then, the Sheriff walked to the car and pulled his gun, pointing it at Mickey. "Back away from those women and lift up your hands!"

"What's the matter, Sheriff? We're just having some fun," said Mickey.

"Sheriff, someone is locked inside the trunk. Mickey has the keys," I said.

The Sheriff looked at Mickey and said, "Give the keys to Sue."

Mickey pulled the keys out of his pocket and threw them at me. I caught the keys with both hands and opened the trunk. Inside the trunk was Alice Shaw. Her mouth was gagged and taped, and her hands were tied behind her back. I took off the gag and said, "Alice, are you okay? Are you hurt?"

"I am okay now."

"What is going on?" asked the Sheriff.

He gave me a knife to cut the ropes from around her arms.

"I was kidnapped by Mickey Slater this morning as I was walking to the conference. He was driving his car and asked if I wanted a ride to the conference. I said, no, I want to walk. Then he said he had information about Anton and would tell me only if I stepped into his car. When I got into the car, he had a knife and said he was going to kill me like he had killed the others. He tied my hands behind my back and put a gag and tape on my mouth. He drove to a deserted road and told me to get out of the car and get into the trunk. He opened the car door and the trunk, and dragged me to the open trunk. I was so scared that I didn't know what to do. He drove away and came to this park. I had no idea where I was. After about thirty minutes I heard two women talking, so I pounded on the door of the trunk."

The Sheriff walked towards Mickey and put handcuffs on his wrists. Then he put his gun back into the holster on his hip.

"Get into the back seat; we're driving to the Police Station. Sue, will you take Alice to the hospital emergency and see if she has any injuries.

"No, I am okay, he didn't hurt me. I would rather ride back with you and press charges against this man," said Alice.

"Anna Marie and I will take Alice to the Police Station. All of us can make a statement," I said.

"I'll call two of my Deputies to pick up the Jaguar and take it to the station," said the Sheriff.

"Wait a minute!" a voice came from the woods. Out walked Sandra Taylor holding a gun. "Sheriff, open the door and let Mickey out and unlock the handcuffs."

As the Sheriff was complying with her demand, he saw the Deputy silently creeping towards Sandra.

The Deputy pointed his gun at her head and said, "Drop your gun." Immediately she dropped her gun. "Put your hands behind you." He took out his handcuffs and put them on Sandra's wrists. "Get into the back seat of the Sheriff's car. You and Mickey will be taken to the Police Station."

"Good job, Deputy."

The Sheriff drove his car out of the park towards Eureka Springs. I followed in my car with Alice sitting in the front seat and Anna Marie sitting in the back seat.

"Alice, why did Mickey kidnap you? Do you know something about them, something criminal?" I asked.

"Yes, Anton told me that he had discovered Arthur Spencer and Mickey Slater were in business together smuggling drugs in antique furniture. He overheard them talking about their drug contacts in Little Rock one evening after a Metaphysical group meeting. He was in the restroom when they walked in. At first they didn't see him

196

sitting in one of the stalls until they saw his shoes. Mickey tried to open the stall, but couldn't. He threatened Anton with his life if he told anyone what he heard. He was afraid to say anything to the police. He had no evidence. After having drinks at Brews on Thursday evening, Mickey put a note in his pocket that said: *Meet me tomorrow night at 9:00 at the Historical Museum.* After Brews, Anton took me to my room and told me about the note. We didn't know what to do. He decided that he would meet with Mickey after the Friday conference."

We arrived at the Police Station in Eureka Springs. I parked the car and we walked into the station. A policeman met us at the door. He asked us to follow him into a private room.

"The Sheriff told me to take you to this room. Please sit down. We would like for each one of you to make a statement about your experiences this morning. Here are some forms and pens. Do any of you want a cup of coffee?"

"Yes," all three of us replied. "Make them black."

For the next thirty minutes we wrote about our experiences. As we completed the writing of our statements, the Sheriff walked into the room and sat down.

"Thanks to all of you, we found our murderers. We put the couple in separate rooms for individual interrogations. When they refused to talk, we left the rooms. The Deputy and I met to discuss what they said. Since neither person confessed, we decided to tell them that the other person had confessed and implicated them in the murders. We went back to the interrogation rooms and said the other person had confessed. That trick worked. Sandra said that Mickey did all the killings. Mickey said that Sandra had helped him. The motive they gave was to keep all the money from the sale of the drugs. They had buried the drugs in the woods at Lake Leatherwood until the buyer could meet them on Sunday afternoon. Anton was murdered because he threatened to go to the police and tell them about the drug smuggling. When Arthur and Clara met Mickey at Lake Leatherwood, the couple wanted a bigger cut of the drug money. Sandra and Mickey decided that they wanted all the money. While Sandra was showing the couple where the drugs were buried, Mickey cut the brake fluid line of their car. When they left Leatherwood Lake the brakes failed going around a mountain curve, and the car and passengers plunged into the deep valley. Mickey and Sandra wanted to kill Alice because they were afraid Anton had told her they were smuggling drugs."

"Sounds like the case is solved," I said to the Sheriff.

"Yes, I want to personally thank you and Anna Marie for helping us solve the case. I do not condone you risking your lives this morning. However, without your help in finding the Jaguar and Alice, the Deputy and I might have arrived too late to save her and arrest the couple."

"I'm glad that we could be of some assistance. Now, that the UFO Conference is over, it's time for us to go back to our motel and check out," I said. Anna Marie and Alice climbed into the car.

We drove to the Inn of the Ozarks and parked near Alice's room.

"Thank you for saving my life. Wait here, I'll go into my room and give you a copy of my presentation," said Alice. When Alice returned, she gave each of us a copy of her presentation.

"Thanks so much," we said to her. "Take care of yourself and best wishes for your future."

We drove back to the Joy Hotel, checked out, and started our drive to Springfield. We stopped in Branson for lunch and continued our drive to our homes to Springfield.

Epilogue

Attending the UFO Conference was worthwhile. I gained some new information that I would like to continue exploring. Identifying murder victims is not something that I look forward to seeing ever again. The images have stayed with me for quite a while. Although, I believe that all of us have past lives, I would rather that we choose when to die, not have someone else end our life before our time.

Characters

Tom, writer, Springfield, Missouri

Sue Henry, telling the story, Springfield, Missouri

Anna Marie, writer and friend of Sue Henry

Members of the Little Rock Metaphysical Group

Joe Weis, leader of Metaphysical Group in Little Rock

Arthur Spencer, Imports & Exports, Little Rock

Clara Spencer, wife of Arthur, Little Rock

Anton Browning, clerk in an Antique Store, Little Rock

Alice Shaw, researcher, Little Rock, friend of Anton

Mickey Slater, Imports & Exports

Sandra Taylor, friend of Mickey Slater

Manager of the Joy Motel

Sheriff

Deputy

Made in the USA
Middletown, DE
26 June 2021